BUT BILLY CAN'T FLY

ANGI FOX
ELLY GRANT

Copyright (C) 2019 by Angi Fox & Elly Grant

Layout design and Copyright (C) 2022 by Next Chapter

Published 2022 by Next Chapter

Edited by Marilyn Wagner

Cover art by CoverMint

Mass Market Paperback Edition

This book is a work of fiction. Names, characters, places, and incidents are the product of the author's imagination or are used fictitiously. Any resemblance to actual events, locales, or persons, living or dead, is purely coincidental.

All rights reserved. No part of this book may be reproduced or transmitted in any form or by any means, electronic or mechanical, including photocopying, recording, or by any information storage and retrieval system, without the author's permission.

CHAPTER ONE

BILLY

"Billy - Billeee, get a move on or you'll miss the bus and pick up that note or you'll forget something."

Mum's voice is irritating, constant, like a fly buzzing too near my face. I want to smack it away, smack it away.

"Can you hear me Billy? Get moving!"

'No gentleness, no kindness, bloody cow,' that's what my Dad used to say, 'Bloody cow.'

He said it one day, when we were in the kitchen. Then he smacked her on the mouth, to stop her nagging voice. He smacked my mum then he left. He ran away, somewhere safe, somewhere far away from the voice, but he didn't take me. He said he would, said he'd come back for me, but he didn't.

"Billee, will you please leave now?" the voice demands.

My mum is driving me mad. She's driving me nuts. She simply has no idea how important my work is. I have to cross the city sometimes four or five times a day carrying important papers. She just has no idea. Every morning I come down to breakfast and the dreaded note is there propped up against the milk jug, waiting for me, it's worrying. She seems to think I can make time to pick up her dry cleaning or get her prescription filled at the chemist. She can't do these things for herself because she's far too busy having tea with Aunty Mabel.

'How on earth do you expect me to keep up to date with what's going on if I don't have a natter with your Aunty Mabel?' she asks. I feel like saying to her, 'Go to the shops and buy a paper or watch the news on the telly,' but of course I don't because she simply has no idea how important my job is or how busy I am. If I try to explain to her, she'll say, 'Don't make a fuss Billy, you're going past there anyway,' and then her eyes fill with tears and she says I don't love her any more. It's not true of course, I do love her because she's my mum and everybody loves their mum. So I pick up the note, as always, and I'll eat my lunch while walking, as always, and I'll miss the morning tea, as always, and Mum never says thank you. At least my boss appreciates me. He knows that without me Henderson's would come to a complete standstill, no-one would get their mail and the work wouldn't get done. In fact, Mr. Henderson often says, 'Billy, you're invaluable.' Invaluable, imagine that, me Billy McDaid, invaluable. He often tells me that, especially if I'm doing him a special favour like making a detour or working a bit late. I don't mind helping him out, at least he appreciates me. Mum has no idea.

I'll be going to Clarkston today with a delivery for Brannigan's. All the way to the West End just to pick up a letter then all the way back to two bus stops from my house, typical. Melanie lives in Clarkston, somewhere. She's always on the bus when it reaches my stop. She's beautiful. Sometimes I ask her the time or talk about the weather and she always says, 'Oh Billy, not again,' as if she's annoyed, but I know that's just her way. I know she really doesn't mind. She likes me. Everyone likes me. I'm invaluable.

I step outside into the rain and pull the door shut. The rain cools my hot cheeks and I breathe out with a loud sigh and head for the bus stop. As I turn the corner into Nethervale Avenue, Stamperland becomes Netherlee. I like this street with its pretty bungalows and tidy gardens. They remind me of dolls' houses. Lovely little houses, cleanly painted with lovely little gardens full of colourful flowers, homes for lovely families with smiling faces. It's like a picture from a cartoon and I wish I could stay here forever and be part of it.

Well, enough of this daydreaming, I say to myself. I'm almost at the bus stop, time to concentrate on the job in hand, time to don my Henderson's hat as Mr Henderson would say. I hope Melanie's on the bus, she's so beautiful and I look forward every morning to seeing her. She looks exactly like Pamela Anderson from Baywatch. I'd love to sit beside her, but when she sees me getting, on she puts her bag on the seat and spreads herself out so there's no room. I don't suppose she likes company first thing in the morning or after work when she's tired. I always try to find a seat behind her so I can watch her without her noticing me and, if I'm lucky enough, there'll be a seat directly behind her then I can smell her perfume and, if I'm very gentle, I can touch her lovely hair and she doesn't notice.

I wish I had a girlfriend like Melanie but I know my mum wouldn't approve.

'I don't approve, Billy,' she'd say. 'That girl is nothing but a tart, a common little slut,' she'd say.

Mum thinks all beautiful young women are sluts and that's because of the 'incident' with Molly Gibson. I know Molly was thirty-seven and I was only sixteen, but she wasn't hurting me, I liked the things we were doing together, she was soft and gentle. I liked touching her. She said I was handsome and built like an ox. She said she was lonely and her husband didn't know how to love her. Her bedroom was pink and soft and fluffy like candy-floss and her bed smelled like flowers, but it was probably 'Febreze.' Mum uses 'Febreze' on my trainers and it smells the same. It was terrible when Mum came in with Molly's husband. It was so embarrassing. Mum started shrieking, calling her a whore and a slut. She said I was a poor, simple soul who didn't have the brainpower to know any better. It was so embarrassing. Then Mum dragged me out of the house with my clothes unbuttoned and my shoes in my arms. Molly was crying and I began to cry too. Poor Molly had to move house and her husband left her, just like Dad left us. Mum shouldn't have interfered. It was all her fault. It's always her fault.

I'm first in line at the bus shelter. I like being first in line because I can see everything coming along without someone's head getting in the way. Mr. Henderson will drive past soon in his blue Mercedes. Mum always says, 'He should stop and give you a lift, Billy. Stuck-up snob thinks he's better than us, but he isn't. I remember wee Johnny Henderson when he was running about with dirty knees and snot dripping from his nose. He's no better than us. My father used to help his father home from the pub you know. His father was always drunk.' Then she gets that look on her face and snorts. 'I went to primary school with Johnny Henderson you know.' I say nothing because I don't know if I should answer her. Mum forgets that Mr. Henderson gave me a job when I was having trouble finding one. She's got a very short memory when it suits her. Anyway, I know he doesn't give me a lift because it wouldn't be appropriate. He explained that to me and I understand. I wish my mum would try to understand. Besides, if he stopped for me, he'd have to stop for everyone. He'd have to pick up Melanie and that definitely wouldn't be appropriate. You know what office gossip is like, everyone would talk about it. 'Mr. Henderson is having an affair with Melanie,' they'd say. 'Dirty old man should know better,' they'd say. And it wouldn't be true, but they wouldn't care and it would be terrible and Melanie would have to leave.

    I feel my eyes fill with tears and I know I have to stop thinking about it. Mum says when I get melancholy, I must think only good thoughts and the sadness will go away. So I think about Molly and her pink, fluffy bedroom and I can almost feel her hands touching my private place. It makes me feel good inside. It makes me feel warm, and I wish the bus would hurry up and come, so I can sit behind Melanie and smell her perfume and, maybe if I'm lucky, touch her pretty hair.

CHAPTER TWO

MELANIE

"That skirt's a bit short for the office, Melanie. Hadn't you better change?"

Here we go again, I think. Why can't Mum say, just for once, 'You look lovely, Mel, you're pretty, Mel, have a nice day, Mel?'

"I've worn it several times before Mum, nobody's commented."

"I bet the men like it," she says, scornfully. "Your top is a bit low cut too. If you bend over in that skirt, they'll see your knickers."

"They might if I was wearing any," I mutter, too quietly for her to hear.

She's just jealous because she's stuck here, a bored, middle-aged, dried-up housewife, while I'm young, free and single. The truth is, it doesn't need to be this way for her. I'm an adult now, all grown up. She could tidy herself up, go to college and learn some new skills. Get a job. Get a life. She's only forty-two, surely there's something she could be doing instead of nagging me. Mind you, I suppose it's much easier for me to get on in the world. I'm only twenty-two, I'm in my prime. I have stunning looks, a great body and I know how to use them. It's much easier and quicker to get to the top when you're beautiful, not that I don't have brains as well, you understand. My mum simply doesn't have a clue about such things. She just has no idea.

It certainly worked for me with Alan, the office manager. You'd think a married man would have more experience, be less naïve, and yet it was so easy to reel him in. He was a pushover. His brains are in his pants, what a jerk. I waited until lunch time, until the other girls in the typing pool were out of the office.

"Alan," I said, smiling and fluttering my eyelashes. "I have to put some papers on the high shelf in the filing cupboard and I'm afraid of heights. Would you come with me and hold the ladder, please?" Then I smoothed my skirt with my hands showing off the shape of my bum and the fact that the skirt barely covered it. Alan licked his lips in anticipation.

"Of course I'll help you, Melanie," he agreed, as I knew he would. Got you, I thought to myself, now you'll belong to me.

He followed me to the cupboard and I knew that he was walking behind me so he could watch me move. I didn't let him down. I swung my hips provocatively then, when we were almost at the cupboard, I looked over my shoulder, gave him my best smile and I winked at him. He followed like a dog after a bitch on heat. He was practically panting when I climbed the ladder to reach the shelf. I positioned myself on the top of the small ladder then stepped one foot forward to rest on a ledge. My legs were spread wide open and of course my tight skirt rode right up over my bare thighs. Alan's nose was level with the top of my leg. He only had to glance up to realise I wasn't wearing any underwear and he didn't let me down. His face was as red as a beetroot and, for a moment, I thought he was embarrassed and I'd gone too far.

Then he said, "Oh God, Melanie, you're so beautiful," and I knew then his red face was from lust not embarrassment. "Please may I kiss your lovely lips?" he begged in a throaty sort of voice.

"Oh, yes Alan, I'd love that," I gasped, as if overcome with passion.

When you're good, you're good, and I'm the best. I was about to step down when he suddenly buried his face in my crotch and I felt his tongue darting about. It was quite a surprise. Oh, those lips, I thought, maybe he's not as naive as I'd imagined. Men are so easy when you know how to manipulate them and Alan was no exception. That little fling has given me a lot of power. He was so easy to reel in, a pushover really.

"Melanie, you're going to be late. You'd better get a move on."

Mum's voice interrupts my chain of thought.

"It's all right, Mum," I reply. "Alan's my boss and he doesn't mind if I'm a bit late. He'll cover for me because I'm so good at my job."

As I step through the door, I see it's raining. Damn, damn, damn, my hair will get wet and I'm going out with Ben later. I risk missing the bus and run back for my umbrella. I must look my best tonight. Ben drives a Porsche and his father owns a furniture warehouse, he'll take me somewhere good, like Sparkle's Nightclub. Footballers and pop stars go there when they're in Glasgow. It is THE place to be seen. I might meet someone really important so I've got to look my absolute best. After all, just because I'll be arriving with Ben, doesn't mean I have to leave with him.

Oh no, there's the bus. I'll have to run. It's moving slowly, the doors are open, phew, just made it, lucky the driver waited for me. I won't be late after all. I sit on my seat and try to catch my breath. We're nearly at Billy's stop. If I lay my umbrella on the seat next to mine, that gormless moron won't be able to sit beside me. I can move it if someone good looking, or at least normal, gets on. Actually, Billy is quite good looking, tall and muscular with the bluest eyes and the blondest hair. If it wasn't for the emptiness in those blue eyes I might even fancy him. If only he had Alan's brains and Ben's money, but as he is, he makes my skin crawl. I wish he wouldn't talk to me because someone might think I actually know him. I'm sure he sits behind me so that he can watch me and sometimes I can feel him touching my hair. Ugh, he gives me the creeps.

Here he comes now, he never misses the bus. I suppose he's been taught to carry out simple tasks mechanically. I suppose it's the sort of thing they teach at those special schools. I'll look out of the window and pretend not to see him then maybe he'll walk past me. At least the seat directly behind me is already taken. Thank goodness.

"Hello Melanie".

Oh God, here we go. I won't talk, I'll just nod.

"Nice weather, not too cold."

"If you like the rain, I personally hate it."

Oh no, I've done it now. Stupid, stupid, stupid, I've spoken to him now I'll never get rid of him.

"I saw Mr. Henderson drive past in his blue Mercedes," he says.

I nod at him then return to looking out of the window. Maybe he'll get the message. Oh, go away, I think. Walk on. Find a seat at the back of the bus, far away from me. Why doesn't he move stupid, gormless moron? I wish Mr. Henderson would give me a lift in the mornings, he drives right past my door. I know he fancies me. He probably doesn't trust himself. I bet the dirty old sod is just dying to put his hands up my skirt or inside my blouse. His wife's on the same Cancer Research Committee as Mum. She seems quite nice, but all men would stray, given half the chance. When the time is right, when I'm in a position to gain something from him, I'll give him that chance. It won't be so bad. I'll just shut my eyes and pretend he's Brad Pitt. He's about the same age and build. It shouldn't be difficult and besides, it won't last long, these old guys never do.

CHAPTER THREE

BILLY

"Right Billy, these are your deliveries for the morning. I suggest you make Brannigan's your first call, then work your way back to the office."

Betty has sorted out my mail run for me, she always keeps me right. I give her my best smile. Mum always says, 'A smile costs nothing Billy, but it's worth more than gold.'

"You might like a wee cup of tea before you start," Betty adds. "The kettle's just boiled and I've brought you a cake, it's in the bag on the table."

I wish my Mum was more like Betty. She's always kind to me and she smiles a lot and she bakes me cakes to have with my tea. Mum never lets me have sugar in my tea because she says it makes me too excitable. Betty says I'm sweet with or without sugar, but she always puts two spoonfuls in anyway. I love my work. I have a briefcase with a lock and a special key that I keep on my keyring. I'm the only person who gets to open the case. Some of the documents I deliver are top secret and I'm in charge of them. If only Mum would understand how important my job is, she wouldn't ask me to run her stupid errands.

When I reach Brannigan's, I place my briefcase on Susan's desk and open it with my special key.

"Hiya Billy, what have you got for us today? Something secret?" Susan asks, and she smiles and winks at Clare.

"Of course, it's secret," I answer, "Otherwise I wouldn't have to keep it under lock and key."

"Will you trust me to give it to Mr. Caldwell, Billy, or do you have to deliver it personally?" Clare asks, returning Susan's wink.

"I suppose I can trust you," I answer. "But you'll have to sign for it, of course."

"Of course," Clare says.

"Of course," mimics Susan, and they both giggle. I really like Susan and Clare. They're very friendly and so efficient.

"So, Billy," Clare asks. "Have you got yourself a girlfriend? It's nearly St. Valentine's Day."

"Of course I have. Of course I have a girlfriend. All men have girlfriends," I reply.

I know I've told a lie. I don't really have a girlfriend, but I could have. Melanie could be my girlfriend. She likes me. Everybody likes me.

"What's her name then, Billy?" Clare asks.

"Is she pretty?" Susan asks.

"Have you kissed her yet?"

"Does she live near you?"

Too many questions, I can't think straight.

"Her name's Melanie," I reply. "Melanie Coulson. She lives near here, in Clarkston. She's beautiful. She looks just like Pamela Anderson from Baywatch."

"Oh really," Clare says.

"Is that right?" Susan adds, "Whereabouts, in Clarkston?"

"I can't remember the street name, but I know where it is. I could show you if I wasn't working."

"Is it Melanie Coulson from Hillview Drive?" Susan questions. "I think I went to school with her. Wasn't she going out with Ben, 'the Porsche'?"

Clare has now signed for the document so I close my briefcase and leave without answering. Too many questions, I can't think straight. When I step outside, my mind begins to clear. I've told a lie. Melanie isn't my girlfriend yet. I've told a lie. God will punish me. I must send her a Valentine card and explain that I want her to be my girlfriend. That'll make it all better. I could buy one at the newsagent's across the road. If I follow her home after work, I can see where she lives, then I'd know where to send the card. I'd know her address.

After I buy the card, my next call is to deliver court documents to Mr. Stevens, so I get the bus back towards town. I sit beside a lady soldier. She's an old lady with grey hair but she's wearing a uniform like a soldier. She has a hat and lots of badges on her jacket. She keeps staring at me and she doesn't smile. Maybe she knows I've told a lie about Melanie. Mum always says, 'Billy, when you tell a lie, it's written all over your face.'

I lean across the lady to look at my reflection in the window. I can't see any writing on my face.

"Do you mind?" the lady soldier says. "Please keep to your own seat."

I apologise and clutch my briefcase to my chest. If only she knew I was carrying top secrets. If only she knew how important my job was, she might not be so grumpy. Surely a lady soldier would understand.

When I get off the bus, I'm relieved the lady soldier stays on because she makes me feel uncomfortable. I wonder if she's got a gun in her handbag, like they have on the telly? I wonder if she could arrest someone for telling lies? I hope I don't meet her again. She frightens me.

CHAPTER FOUR

BELLA

I am so glad that man got off the bus. He really was most strange, leaning across me like that. I wonder what on earth he was up to. I didn't give him a second glance at first. I thought he was normal at first, until I saw those blank eyes and his slack jaw. Poor retarded soul, clutching his briefcase as if it held diamonds.

We mustn't call them retarded these days because it's no longer appropriate it seems. Now we use euphemisms like, 'learning difficulties' or 'special needs'. It makes no difference, in my book they're still retarded, whatever they're called. In my day, people like him were put into institutions. They certainly weren't allowed out on their own and, looking at him, I can understand why. He was so big and at first glance, looked quite normal. A young person might be fooled into thinking he was normal and that could be very dangerous. Mabel, my housekeeper, has a friend with a retarded son but he's never around when she calls on her. He probably goes to one of those special schools.

My WRVS ladies have seen it all before in our old boys as they struggle with their memories. But these boys are at the end of their lives, having fought for Queen and Country. They deserve our consideration and our care. After all, they've lost limbs fighting in the war to ensure our freedom. Some of these poor old soldiers live in abject poverty and, without the WRVS, wouldn't even have company once a week. It's a damned disgrace. On the other hand, these 'special needs' people drain money and resources their entire lives and give nothing back except heartbreak to their poor mothers.

At last, time to get off this bus. I hate travelling by bus. It's full of common people. They're dirty and they smell and they have no choice but to travel this way. I, on the other hand, can afford a taxi but why should I pay the price? I pay my taxes like everyone else. I'm entitled to use public transport. Besides, if the rich didn't use the public transport system it would cease to exist, then what will poor people do? Walk, that's what they'd have to do, out in all weathers, exposed to the elements, they'd have no choice. That's why I insist all my ladies travel by public transport, it's our civic duty. They might not like my rules but they will damn well respect them. People always respect strong leadership and discipline, which is the reason why I insist the officers get served their tea first.

As I open the door to the community hall, a blast of heat hits my face. Judith's got the heating up too high again, it will drain the resources. Why on earth do we bother to knit blankets for the old boys if she is going to turn this room into a furnace? And there isn't a single window open, no ventilation. This place smells like an old army boot. Just because I'm half an hour later than usual, all Hell's broken loose.

"Judith, Judith," I call. Where is that girl?

"I'm here Mrs. Worthington," she replies, standing up from behind a tea trolley.

"Get the heating turned down and get a window open at once. Now, let's sort out the teas. There are far too many biscuits on that plate Ethel, only one for each remember and none for Frederick or Peter because they're diabetic. You've got fifteen biscuits there and there should only be nine. Don't give the cup to Charlie, Grace. Can't you see he's got Parkinson's disease? Do you want him to shake the tea all down his front? Hold the cup for him, Dear. Yes, you hold the cup."

I don't know, I just don't know. This place would fall apart without me. These young volunteers have no idea how to run this unit. Most of them weren't even born during the war. They're lucky I can afford to give up my valuable time to train them.

"Mrs. Worthington, Mrs. Worthington, come quickly please."

"What now, Grace? Why are you shouting? What's all the panic? Can't you see I'm busy?"

"It's Bill, Mrs. Worthington. I think he's D E A D!"

"Why are you spelling, you stupid girl? They are old, not illiterate. You should know the procedure by now. Wheel him into the kitchen and we'll check him over. Ethel spread some papers on the floor. Judith, fetch the mirror. We must make absolutely sure because Grace has got it wrong before. She thought Charlie was dying last month and he was only choking on a biscuit. Lift his head. Hold that mirror steady. It's not misting and from the smell of him, I would say you were right this time Grace. Stop blubbering, Dear, he had a good innings. You had better call an ambulance and tell them to come to the rear entrance. Oh, and Judith, tell them not to put on those ridiculous sirens and flashing lights. I don't want them upsetting the others because it takes ages to settle them, once they're excited."

While we are waiting, I allow myself a private thought. Bill said only last week he was going to leave me a thousand pounds in his will. So I think I'll treat myself to the coat I've been admiring in Frasers. Bill's daughter would never contest the will. She was so pleased when I took him off her hands once a week. She'll be even happier now he's gone for good.

"Mrs. Worthington, Mrs. Worthington," Judith interrupts my train of thought.

"What now, girl?"

"Charlie has just eaten two biscuits."

"That's all right dear. Bill won't be wanting his now."

CHAPTER FIVE

BILLY

When I get to the court there's a gang of dangerous looking boys standing outside. They're wearing black jackets and baggy denims and they have shaved heads and earrings in their noses. Some of them have tattoos on their heads and I find them very frightening. I think they must be criminals waiting to go into court and I don't want to walk past them in case they start with me. Mum always says, 'If in doubt, don't do it, Billy,' and I have doubts, serious doubts.

I decide to walk round the building once to see if they go away, but as I walk, I begin to worry. I'm going to be late for my appointment with Mr. Stevens. I'm going to be late delivering the document. What will I do? What will I do? When I arrive back at the entrance, they're still there, I'll have to walk past them.

"Hey there, fuckwit. What's in the case? Hey, fuckwit, I'm talking to you."

They're blocking my way. I don't know what to do. They're closing in around me.

"What's in the case, moron? Can we have a look?"

"Come on, you big dope, let's have a look."

I'm frightened. Can't think. Can't think straight. What would Superman do? Superman would fly over their heads, right into the court building and they wouldn't be able to touch him. But I can't fly. One of them is pulling at my arm. What will I do? What will I do? His nose is practically touching mine and his breath smells stinky. It smells of smoke and alcohol. I need help. Why won't someone help me? There's a policeman outside the court. A policeman could help me.

"Help. Help," I shout. "Come and help me, Mr. Policeman."

The gang draws back from me. I've got some power now. They're scared of me when I shout.

"Help, Mr. Policeman. Come and help me."

The policeman starts to slowly walk towards me.

"Yes, Sir," he says. "What seems to be the matter? Are you in trouble?"

"I need to get into the court to find Mr. Stevens. I've got a delivery for him."

"And what seems to be the problem, Sir?"

I look around at the gang. They're staring at me. Best to say nothing, I think.

"N no problem, Mr. Policeman, I'll go in now," I say, and I run to the entrance.

When I enter the court building, Mr. Steven's secretary jumps out at me.

"Thank goodness you're here, Billy. Mr. Stevens has been like a bear with a sore head this morning. The old bastard is so bad tempered. Give me the papers, quickly."

I stand for a minute, trying to take in what she's said.

"The papers, Billy, the papers. For God's sake,

open the damn briefcase, Mr. Stevens is in a terrible mood and he's in a hurry."

I open my case with my special key and the secretary lifts the papers out of it. Then she quickly flicks through them.

"Thank God, Billy, these are the right ones. Bye now. See you," she says and she rushes away.

She hasn't signed for them. What will I do? She hasn't signed for them. I go to the policeman at the door and explain to him what's happened. He looks at me for a moment then he says, "Give me your form and I'll sign for it, Sir. If you have any problem, just refer it back to me."

He smiles. I'm so relieved. I've got a signature on my form, now I can go to my next call and I won't get into trouble.

I come out of the court building and walk round the corner. There's a noise behind me of running footsteps and shouting. Before I get a chance to turn around to see what's happening, I am slammed against a wall and my briefcase is snatched from my hand. I'm being pushed this way and that, I'm being banged off the wall and slapped. There's shouting and I don't know what's happening.

"Hey fuckwit. Thought you'd got away, didn't you?"

"Thought you were smarter than us, moron."

"What's in the case then? Let's have a look."

"Yeah, what's in the case?"

"Give me back my case," I plead. "It's got secrets in it. Top secrets. You're not allowed to see them."

"Mmm, top secrets, is it? Are you a spy then?"

"Nah, he's not a spy, he's a moron."

"I can't get the fucking thing open. Give us the fucking key, moron."

"There's nothing left in it," I lie. "I've made all my calls."

"Well if it's empty you won't mind us looking in it. Give us the fucking key!"

One of the gang produces a knife and begins to work at the lock but it won't open. They keep pushing me this way and that way and I want to smack them. I want to smack them away, but Mum's words come rushing back to me. 'Remember Billy, you're a big boy. You can't push people because if you push them, you could seriously hurt them.' "If I push you, I'll seriously hurt you," I say. They all stare at me for a moment. "I could kill you, you know. I'm much bigger than you." I'm feeling stronger. I think they're a bit frightened because I'm big.

The one with the knife steps forward and presses it against my cheek. He has the word 'hate' tattooed into his scalp.

"Oh yes, you are bigger than me but I've got this," he says. "I could take your eye out in a second."

I'm scared, my eyes are watering and I need the toilet.

"What's your name, fuckwit?"

I say nothing.

"Tell me your name, moron, or I'll cut you."

"My name is Billy," I reply.

"Well Billy, why isn't your briefcase monogrammed? It hasn't got your name on it. How do we know it's yours? You might have nicked it."

A tear runs down my cheek. People are walking past, they see what's happening but nobody is helping me. Why won't they help me? I want to be away from here. I want to be away.

"I'm going to be very kind to you, Billy," says the boy with the knife. "I'm going to monogram your case for you."

He begins to pick out letters with the knife on the polished leather.

"There we are, it's got your name on it now," he says, and the other gang members laugh. He holds the case in front of my eyes and I can see that he has scratched the word 'moron' into the leather. My beautiful case is ruined. What will I tell Mr. Henderson? Lots of tears run down my face and I feel very sad.

"Now," says the boy with the knife. "I think we'll put your name on your forehead. Then everyone will know who you are."

He holds the knife near my face and I feel sick.

"What are you up to lads?" a voice from behind them calls.

I see someone coming towards me. He's a big boy and he's wearing a school blazer. "What's going on here?" he asks.

"Ah, we're just having a bit of fun with this moron," says the boy with the knife.

"Yeah, he's a fuckwit," says one of the others.

"I know him," says the boy in the blazer. "He works for my uncle at Henderson's. You're Billy, aren't you?" he asks. I look into his face and I vaguely recognise him.

"Y y yes, I'm Billy," I stammer.

"Yeah, he's one of my uncle's workers. Let him go lads."

"Aw come on Jez. We're just having a bit of fun."

"No, I said let him go. He works for my uncle. Family is family, you know what I mean?"

"You're a lucky moron," one of them rasps in my ear and shoves the briefcase back into my arms.

"Can I go now?" I ask the boy in the blazer.

"Yeah, get on your way Billy, they'll not bother you anymore."

I am so relieved. I am so grateful. I want to say something nice to the boy in the blazer so that he knows how I feel.

"You're just like James Bond," I tell him when I walk past him. "Thank you for saving me." As I walk away, I hear them all laughing.

"James Bond eh? Shaken not stirred."

"A big dick with a Scottish accent. Yeah that sounds like you, Jez!"

I walk on quickly in case they change their minds about letting me go and they keep laughing as I walk away.

CHAPTER SIX

JEZ

"What are you doing here, boys? Not like you to be hanging about the court."

"We're waiting for the wimmin. Donna-Marie and Kelly are up for shoplifting again."

"Think they'll get the jail?"

"Nah, they're only fifteen. Slap on the wrist."

"When did you get the tattoo, Derek?" I ask.

"Last week. Didn't cost me a penny. Tony did it with a needle and Indian ink. I was going to have the word 'dangerous' but my head's not big enough, so we went for 'hate' instead."

"Aye and Derek pierced my ear for me with a darning needle and a potato. Now I can get rings all the way up," says Tony.

"Cher wants her nipples done. Do you think you could do them?" I ask.

"I'll do it with my teeth," volunteers Tam and they all laugh.

"Not a chance," I reply. "She'd enjoy it too much."

"And where is the lovely Cher?" Derek asks.

"She's chained to a tree in Craigie Park, protesting against the motorway. I'm taking her something to eat later. The bulldozers aren't actually coming till tomorrow but she's seeing how long she can last without needing a pee. It's a sort of trial run. I've got the key to the handcuffs here," I say, holding it aloft.

"What happens if she needs to go before you get back?"

"Well the way I see it is this," I reply. "She's in a park next to a tree, if it's all right for a dog, it's all right for her."

Derek asks, "Where did you get the handcuffs?"

"Oh, I've had them for ages. Cher likes me to use them when we're having sex. I bought them for a fiver at the Barras market. What's new with you lads?" I ask.

"Did you hear about Willie Caldwell, Jez?"

"No, who's Willie Caldwell?"

"That red-haired geezer who runs the bookie shop."

"Oh yes, I know who you mean. What's happened to him then?"

"His wife caught him in bed with his twelve-year-old stepdaughter. She went ballistic. I wouldn't care but everyone's been with that wee lassie, it's nothing new. Anyway, to cut a long story short, so to speak," Derek says and the others laugh.

"Not to put too fine a point on it," Tony adds, and they laugh even harder.

"No point on it at all," offers Tam.

"Jesus, will you stop laughing and get on with the story," I say.

"Well," says Derek. "His wife waited till he was asleep then did a 'Bobbit' on him with a kitchen knife. She cut his dick clean off then she ran into the street, screaming. The poor bastard nearly died. They had to rush him to the Royal where some wog doctor sewed it back on. Imagine knowing that some wog had been touching your dick."

"What do you think will happen to the wife?" I ask

"Some smart bitch lawyer will get her off. They'll say it was PMT. They'll call it diminished responsibility. She was probably just jealous that the young lassie was getting it and she wasn't."

"Now neither of them will get any," Tony adds. "My wee sister's in the same class at school as the lassie. She says all the weans are calling him Frankenstein's Willie."

"Anyway Jez, what are you doing here?" Tam asks. "Not in school today? Won't Sir be missing you?" he taunts.

"He's a pervy old bastard, that teacher of yours," says Derek. "He worked in some wog country for years. They'll shag anything that moves in those countries."

"Ma sister works for his folks," says Tam. "They're Jews, you know. They live in a big mansion in Whitecraigs and they've got bags of money. It makes you wonder why that weirdo lived in a commune. That must tell you something, Jez."

"Sir probably is missing me, but I don't give a shit. I'll write myself a note. My folks are away again and it's easy to forge the housekeeper's signature. That brings me to the reason why I've been looking for you guys. The housekeeper is going to her sister's on Saturday and staying overnight. My parents are paying her a fortune to look after the house and cook for me and the old bat is sneaking off. She said she's going to trust me to look after myself for the night. I can't let her down, can I lads?"

"No, you can't let her down, Jez," says Tony

"Certainly not," adds Tam.

"So what time is the party?" asks Derek.

"Well, I thought it should start about ten. That will give everyone a chance for a few drinks before they arrive. So I'll be needing some help lads. How much booze can you get your hands on?"

"That depends on how much money you've got," Derek replies.

"I've always got money," I reply. "You know I've never let you down."

"Well then, the sky's the limit. Tell us what you want."

"Enough to last fifty people all night and of course I'll also need some E's and some Coke. Wholesale for resale."

"Aye, no bother Jez. I take it we're the guests of honour?"

"Of course lads and don't forget to bring your women if they get out by the weekend."

"Will Cher be bringing her tree with her? She'll be quite attached to it by then," jokes Tony.

"Or maybe you could transfer her to the bed post and she could protest against male domination instead"

"I bet she's a bit of a goer," says Derek. "I wouldn't mind a piece of that action myself!"

"Is that right Derek?" I ask. "And do you think you're up to it?"

The idea of watching Cher and Derek together quite turns me on, especially if she's handcuffed to the bed and it's against her will. She's such a snob, she'd hate someone like Derek even breathing her air. She'd scream the bloody place down. The thought gets more attractive by the minute.

"I tell you what, Derek," I say. "I'll swap you half an hour with Cher for ten tabs of E, but only if I can watch. Have we got a deal?"

"Certainly. If you're sure," Derek readily agrees.

"What about me, Jez?" asks Tony. "Can I get the same deal?"

"No, I don't think so, Tony. For you it would be a case of Scotch."

"Done." says Tony. "I can nick that in no time."

"What about me?" asks Tam. "Can I get a bit of action too?"

"Nah, you're too ugly. It would do nothing for me to watch you with her."

"Aw come on, Jez. I'll give you 20 tabs of E."

"Oh well, OK, as you've twisted my arm. It's probably your only chance of a shag this year."

"Here come the wimmin now," Derek observes. "What did you get," he asks them.

"Slap on the wrist and we've to report to a probationer for six months," replies Kelly.

"Never mind, hen, Jez is having a party on Saturday night. That should cheer you up."

"Right, Donna-Marie, I need you to lift me a case of Scotch for a wee deal I've got going with Jez here," Tony says, winking at me. "So c'mon down to the supermarket."

"I'll need some cash to get stuff," Derek says to Kelly. "So I'll need you to go with those two old guys tonight. That should just about cover it."

"I'd rather go with Jez," she says with a leer.

"Don't be stupid, Kelly. He's got a woman. He doesn't need to pay for it."

After saying my goodbyes, I head back towards school, back to my other life. Now I've sorted out my supplies, I'll need to round up some paying customers for the party. Money is power and I have the means to make it. Unlike my stupid parents who spend their entire lives in the boardroom or on a plane, I can sit in the comfort of my own home and watch the dosh flow in. The secret is to give the people what they want, or what they think they want. At the rate I'm going, I'll be a millionaire by the time I'm twenty. I've already got the money for my Jaguar safely stashed. All I need now is the driving licence. Yes another few years and I can kiss the scum goodbye. Then I'll live in the South of France with the rest of the beautiful people.

CHAPTER SEVEN

BILLY

As I walk along the pavement, I look at my damaged case and I can't stop crying. Hot tears wet my cheeks and my nose is running. My clothes are stuck to me with sweat and I feel sick. I have one more call to make, but I'm too upset to care if I'm late. As I pass Burger King, I feel I have to go in and use the toilet as I don't think I can make it to my next call. The 'Gents' is completely empty and I'm relieved because it embarrasses me to go in front of anyone. Afterwards, I wash my hands and soak my face in the cold water. It makes me feel much better. When I pass through the restaurant to leave, the smell of the fried food makes me really hungry. So although I'm now late for my next appointment, I hear myself ordering a burger and fries, then realise too late that I no longer have the exact change for the bus. I'm definitely going to be late now, very late. While I sit at a table eating my food, I carefully turn my case down on my lap so I don't have to look at the word carved into it. Then I leave the restaurant and walk as quickly as I can.

My last call is at a rich boys' school in the West

End. The school is planning an extension and Henderson's is handling the loan for them. Mr. Henderson told me all about it. It's very important to him because it's his old secondary school. When I enter the playground, I can see that the boys are wearing the same sort of blazers as the boy who rescued me. My horrible experience suddenly comes flooding back to me and hot tears spill out from my eyelids and stream down my face. I'm sobbing loudly and I feel ashamed and embarrassed, but I can't stop. One of the boys stares at me for a moment then disappears into the building, only to reappear again with a man.

"Come with me please," the man says, and he takes me by the arm and leads me into a small office just inside the main door of the school. He offers me a chair and I sit down. Then he hands me a paper hanky to wipe my eyes.

"What seems to be the matter? Are you hurt?" he asks.

I'm sobbing so hard I can't answer, so I just hold up my case and show him the damage. When he sees my case, his face falls and he looks sad. He pulls a chair over beside me and puts his arm around my shoulders.

"That was a cruel and terrible thing for somebody to do. When you feel better, we can talk about it if you'd like."

"The boy had a knife," I say. "He said he was going to cut me. Then a big boy in a blazer came and saved me. He was just like James Bond."

The man smiles kindly. "Go on," he says.

"The boy was from this school. He had the same type of blazer. He was very brave. He saved my life."

"From this school, eh? And where did this happen?"

"Outside the court building. I've just come from the court. I've just made a delivery to Mr. Stevens."

"It sounds as if he was quite a hero, this boy. I just wonder what he was doing out of school."

"Saving me," I offer. "That's what he was doing, he was saving me. I've got a delivery," I say, suddenly remembering. I take out my special key, open my case and hand an envelope to the kind man. "You'll have to sign my form."

"Of course. No problem," he replies. "Now how about a cup of tea to make you feel better?"

"Have you got any chocolate biscuits? I like chocolate biscuits."

"I'm sure I can rustle one up for you."

I munch my chocolate biscuit and drink my tea. I like this room, it's warm and it smells of polish. There are bookshelves all the way up to the ceiling and there's a thick carpet on the floor. The man was right, I do feel much better.

"Now then, let's see if I can't do something to fix this case for you. I'll be back in a few minutes. Don't go away."

He soon comes back carrying a piece of material that looks like leather. It's almost the same colour as my case. He peels a backing off it then sticks it over the damaged part.

"There you are," he says. "Not quite as good as new but not bad, not bad at all."

I am so grateful to him that I put my arms round him and give him a hug and kiss him on the cheek. He smiles at me and pats me on the bottom.

"There, there," he says. "You're all right now."

Then I remember my manners.

"Do I owe you any money?" I ask.

"No, nothing," he says, "Except maybe another hug."

I throw my arms round him and kiss his cheek again and he holds me close and pats my bottom again. Just like Mum does when she's happy with me. Then he walks me to the gate and I start walking back towards Henderson's.

CHAPTER EIGHT

DAVID

Simple affection between men, wonderful, I can still feel his kiss lingering on my cheek and his firm buttocks under my hand. How I miss Africa. How I miss my little black boys with their glistening, ebony skin and their gleaming white teeth. Four years of my life, four years working in Africa, making no impact on the poverty or the deprivation. What a waste of my talents. My parents warned me it would be like that and, on this occasion, they were right, not that I'd tell them, certainly not, I wouldn't give them the satisfaction. They have never tried to understand my needs. They didn't understand when I joined the Jesus Army. My mother cried and wailed and spoke to the Rabbi's wife and my father disinherited me. They didn't understand when I sold the car they gave for my twenty-first birthday and bought a Harley. Neither did they understand when I sold the Harley and bought a motor-home to tour Europe with a group of like-minded, new age travellers. So I shouldn't have been surprised when they didn't understand my VSO work in Africa.

Now, at least, they are almost happy, now that I'm

encaged in this fascist hell-hole and enslaved by upper-class dictators to teach their unappreciative brats. Well at least I don't have to go home to Whitecraigs every night. That would be the final torture, forced to sit amongst the antiques and always use coasters under my glass and never wear my shoes in the house. The list of rules is endless. I'd have to listen to my mother complaining and my father making lewd jokes. I couldn't stand it. I would vegetate. I would drown under the constant stream of eligible young ladies, paraded in front of me like prime beef at an auction, chosen, of course, by my mother and deemed suitable, wifely material. They would all resemble Arlene, my perfect brother's perfect wife who, of course, was also chosen by mother. Not to mention their three monstrous children who all look like toads. They, of course, according to mother, are perfect too. I simply couldn't compete. But would I really want to? I don't suppose mother could show ME off. What could she say?

"Aunty Freda, this is my youngest son David, the queer one who lived in a commune, the one who worked in Africa for four years where he developed a penchant for little boys."

Not quite what she would expect from a nice Jewish boy. To mother I will always be Jewish. To mother I will always be heterosexual. You simply don't get Jewish gays. To mother I will, one day, get married and produce grandchildren who will all look like toads.

I make myself a mug of herbal tea and sit by the window to wait for Jez's inevitable return. Wait for the 'hero' to come back to the fold. A smile creases my face, I can't help it. The pleasure of catching that little bastard overwhelms me. For two years he has tormented me with his innuendos and snide remarks. He menaces me. He torments me. I can never prove a thing because I have never actually caught him doing something wrong. I'd love to catch him out. I would love to control him. He is as beautiful as he is cruel and I'd love to possess him. He knows how I feel about him and he taunts me with it. It's his magnetism that I can't resist, it draws everyone to him. Even that retarded man likened him to James Bond, he felt his power too.

Damn! That's the bell ringing and, like Pavlov's dog, I'm forced to obey. Jez is due in my next class and hasn't entered the school gates yet. I've got him. As I make my way down the corridor, the noise from my classroom meets me. I walk softly so the boys don't hear my approach. I can almost taste the detentions, but as I reach for the handle to open the door somehow, by some invisible radar, they become silent before I can enter the room. I push the door open quickly hoping but failing to catch the look-out who has heralded my arrival. I scan the room and, to my total surprise, see Jez sitting in his usual seat, lazily leaning against the wall, his long legs stretched out in the aisle before him. Our eyes meet. He smirks and mouths a kiss and I feel my face reddening with anger and disappointment. His face breaks into a smile and all eyes in the classroom dart from his face to mine. He is goading me. Bastard! Bastard! Bastard!

"Open your books at page fifty-six," I command, my voice steady and confident. I refuse to give the little shit the satisfaction of getting the better of me. This room may not be much, but in this room, I am master.

CHAPTER NINE

BILLY

It's been a terrible day, terrible, terrible, terrible. I'm glad to be at the bus stop. Soon I'll be safely home watching telly and eating my dinner. The queue is already very long and I hope the bus driver has room for me. Melanie is at the front of the queue. She's looking into a mirror and pouting her lips as she puts on her lipstick, red lipstick. She's beautiful. When she catches sight of me looking at her, she throws her head round and flicks her hair turning away from me. I've embarrassed her because I've seen her putting on her make-up. Things will be different when she's my girlfriend, she won't mind me watching her then. As I look along the queue, I can see the teacher who mended my briefcase, he's talking to another man and they're laughing. The man writes something on a piece of paper and hands it to the teacher. The teacher puts the paper in his jacket pocket then pats the pocket and winks at the man. I wonder what the note says. Maybe it's a secret, maybe it's about the new building. He sees me looking at him and he smiles at me. I would like to stand beside him and laugh with him like the other man is doing, but if

I try to move further up the queue someone will complain. So I stay in my place. When I turn round to look for the bus, I see that I'm standing right next to the lady soldier. It gives me a surprise and I jump. She glowers at me and mutters something under her breath. I can't make out what she's saying, but I don't think it's nice. She frightens me. I back away from her and accidentally bump into a boy and he swears at me and pushes me away from him. The lady soldier snorts and shakes her head. She's very scary, like a baddie in a film. Mr Henderson's blue Mercedes drives past and Mr. Henderson nods at me. He nods only at me, nobody else, just me. It makes me feel important and I look up and down the queue to see how many people have noticed. The teacher smiles at me again. He noticed. The bus arrives and the queue shuffles forward. Melanie is the first person to get on.

Suddenly, out of nowhere, a boy in a blazer appears. He doesn't join the queue but instead jumps onto the bus ahead of everyone who is waiting. He doesn't even pay his fare he just nods at the driver and takes a seat. Everyone is moaning and complaining to each other and the lady soldier shakes her fist in the air as if she wants to punch him. The boy is sitting in a window seat and he looks out at the queue of people and laughs. He gives the lady soldier a 'V' sign with his fingers and her face goes red and I think she might explode. I laugh out loud when I realise that it's my boy in the blazer, my hero, my James Bond. I'm pleased he upset the lady soldier because I think she's horrible.

Finally, it's my turn to get onto the bus and there's just enough room for me to stand. Soon I'll be safe at home, eating my dinner and watching telly. I put my hand in my pocket to see if there's a toffee I can suck because the bus sometimes makes me feel sick. My hand touches a piece of paper, it's Mum's note and I suddenly remember I haven't collected her prescription from the chemist. I forgot all about it when I went to buy the Valentine card. Oh no, she'll be angry and she'll shout at me and I'll feel terrible. I've had a terrible day and now tonight will be terrible too. My eyes are full of tears and I wipe them on my sleeve. I look at Melanie but she turns away. I look at the teacher but he's talking to his friend and doesn't see me. The lady soldier's eyes meet mine and she shakes her head. The boy in the blazer salutes me. Nobody can help me. Nobody can comfort me. Please God let Mum forget about the prescription too.

***

It's eight o'clock on Saturday morning and I'm standing on the pavement holding the Valentine card. I've written Melanie's name on the envelope. The street is very long and I don't know which house is hers so I sit on a garden wall at the end of the street while I think about what to do next. After a while the postman comes round the corner with a bundle of mail in his hand. "Morning," he says cheerfully. "Waiting for someone?"

"I've got to deliver this card," I say. "But I can't remember the street number."

"A Valentine eh, who's the lucky girl?"

"Melanie Coulson. I work beside her. She's beautiful," I reply.

"Quite a little firecracker," he agrees. "And you

work with her? Lucky fellow, maybe I can help you, walk with me and I'll show you where she lives."

As we walk, we talk about all sorts of things. The postman is called Frank and he's very friendly. He tells me he often sees Melanie when he makes his deliveries.

"Do you know," he says. "During the summer she sunbathes topless in her back garden at the weekend. I sometimes see her when I make my deliveries. Because the house is a semi you can see right into the back garden."

I don't reply because I don't know what to say.

Frank continues, "One day I called out to her, 'Nice day for getting a suntan' and she sat up and waved. She didn't try to cover up or anything she just sat there in her chair. Then, cool as a cucumber, she leaned across and picked up her suntan oil, opened her legs wide and began to massage oil into her thighs. You can imagine how I felt. I could hardly walk and I was only half way round my delivery route."

"She's beautiful," I say. "Melanie's going to be my girlfriend. I've told her in my card."

"Well you are a lucky fellow," he replies. "She's a babe."

We walk a bit further then he beckons with his thumb.

"This is the house, the one with the red door. Would you mind putting these through the door too? It will save my legs." He hands me a bundle of mail. "Thanks mate. Good luck with Melanie."

I stand and watch as he walks on towards his next delivery. When he's further down the street I begin to look through the mail. There are two letters for Melanie. One is obviously from her bank because its name is printed on the envelope. The other envelope is hand written. Maybe it's a Valentine from someone else, I think. That would never do she must only receive my card or she might choose someone else to be her boyfriend. I slip the handwritten envelope into my pocket and replace it with my card then I quickly walk up the driveway and post the mail through the letter box, then I return to the safety of the street. As it's Saturday and I don't have to work, I head back to my home, back to my room to open Melanie's letter. I'll be able to see who else is writing to her and she'll never know. If it's not from a boy I can re-seal the envelope and deliver it another day. She'll never know.

I walk down the back streets towards my home with Melanie's letter safely tucked into my pocket. The streets are quiet and I meet no one. I cross the road as I come down the hill because I don't want to walk past the dead cat, although it no longer looks like a cat because crows have been pecking at it for over a week now. I wish someone would take it away. Mr. Peters from next door says that nature takes care of its own and it will soon be turned to dust. Some children laid grass and leaves beside the body because there were no flowers but they've disappeared now and I wish that God or nature would hurry up and take the cat.

When I arrive home, I run upstairs to my room, sit on my bed and carefully look at Melanie's letter. It's in a white envelope, the kind that sticks itself shut so it is quite easy for me to tear open the back without ripping it. I'll be able to read it and re-seal it and she'll never know. I slide the letter out and carefully unfold it and read.

'Melanie,

You must know what you ask is impossible. I could never raise that kind of cash without it being noticed. Somebody would find out. Somebody would tell H. You must give me more time. When old man Henderson is out of the office on Tuesday, we can discuss what to do. Until then you'll simply have to wait. Keep your mouth shut or I'll deny everything and you'll have to face the music yourself. Remember, not a word to anyone. A.'

I read the letter again and again trying to make sense of it. I'm not very sure what it means. Is Melanie in trouble? Who is A? And what are they hiding from Mr. Henderson? I don't really understand any of this. All I know is that something is wrong and it involves Melanie. I carefully refold the letter and replace it in the envelope but when I try to re-seal it, it doesn't stick down evenly, so once again I try to open it. This time the envelope rips and I sit staring at the torn pieces. What will I do? I can't give it back now and I can't keep it. I have to get rid of it, but I can't put it in the bin or Mum will find it and I can't burn it because I'm not allowed to play with matches Suddenly, I have an idea. I know where unwanted paper can go. I am tearing the letter and envelope into small pieces as I head for the bathroom. In two flushes and a squirt of bleach it's gone forever and I don't need to think about it anymore.

CHAPTER TEN

MELANIE

It's been over a week since I confronted Alan and he's acting as if nothing had happened. When I first mentioned `the problem', he said he couldn't discuss it in the office but he would write to me. I hope I haven't asked for too much money but I figure he must be earning at least thirty grand a year so it's only a week's pay, petty cash really. And if I really were pregnant, it would be a small price to pay for my silence. When Alan pays up, I'll ask Stephen and Ben for the same amount. If they all pay it will mean a Caribbean cruise on the 'Sun Princess'. Hopefully, Louise will be just as successful. No more self-catering weeks in Torremolinos for us, now we know how to hit the big time, and I'm sure there'll be a sugar daddy or two on board, to buy us little baubles and trinkets which we can pawn for next year's holiday. Men are such pushovers, their brains are in their pants. I just wish I'd thought of this scam years ago. If his letter doesn't arrive by Monday morning, I'll just have to mention `the problem' in front of the typing pool. No one will know what I'm talking about but it will scare the shit out of Alan. He always says his wife is 'so understanding' about him working late. I wonder if she'll understand this. Men are such jerks. They're so stupid and so frightened about being caught, that not one of them will ask to see a positive pregnancy test. They'll just be so relieved to be let off the hook, so relieved when I'm no longer pregnant, they won't realise I never have been. If that moron Billy didn't give me the creeps, I could fuck him as well. I know he fancies me and he never goes anywhere, he never spends any money so he must be worth a mint. I'm sure he'd hand over cash without any trouble at all because he wouldn't risk his Mum finding out. I suppose I could tell him not to kiss me and I could shut my eyes and pretend he's Daniel Craig. No, no, no, what am I thinking about? Ugh! I couldn't bear his hands on me, never mind his dick inside me. I'll speak to Louise maybe she'll go with him, she's not as choosy as me. Mind you, I know he has a serious crush on me because he sent me a cruddy Valentine card. Only a moron would sign it and tell you he wants you to be his girlfriend. And who the hell are Susan and Clare and what does it matter if they think I'm already his girlfriend? I sometimes wonder what goes on in that idiot's head. Then again, maybe he's not so stupid after all, he's not paying £600 for a pregnancy that doesn't exist.

CHAPTER ELEVEN

BILLY

The bus arrives promptly on Monday and as I climb on board, I can see there's an empty seat beside Melanie. She's staring out of the window and hasn't moved her bag across the seat. She seems to be deep in thought. Maybe she's thinking about my Valentine card, maybe she's saving me a seat beside her, but I can't sit beside her and I can't sit behind her. I can't sit anywhere near her because if she looks at my face she'll know. She'll know I read her letter. She'll know I tore it up. She'll know I flushed it with bleach. Then she'll hate me and she won't be my girlfriend. If I keep my distance for a day or two it won't be so bad. Mum always says that when bad things happen, gradually you forget about them until they disappear completely. In a day or two this will disappear completely. In a day or two there won't have been a letter at all and I won't have to worry. So I make my way to the back of the bus and sit down, but I can't take my eyes off Melanie. I can't stop thinking about her. What if she's in trouble? A man should help his girlfriend if she's in trouble. It's no good. I'll never forget about the letter. I have to find out more. I have to help Melanie.

When I arrive at the office, Betty makes me a mug of tea and gives me a chocolate crispy cake and I munch it while she packs my briefcase.

"Mr. Henderson's car wasn't in its special parking place this morning. Is something wrong with it? Is it broken?" I ask.

"There's been some trouble at his sister's house over the weekend and he's been called to sort things out," Betty replies.

I bite another piece of cake and wonder what could have happened. Maybe there's been a fire, maybe the fire engine had to be called. Or maybe a burglar broke in to steal things and the police are there. Or maybe something bigger has happened like a plane falling on the house or maybe a U.F.O. landing in the garden. I wish I knew. I wish I knew what has happened. It must be important if Mr. Henderson had to go there.

"Where is the house?" I ask.

"Somewhere on the south side, near where you live, Billy".

Well, I think to myself, it can't be a plane crash or I'd have seen it. I pop the last bit of crispy cake into my mouth and wonder some more about what the 'trouble' could be.

Suddenly there is a hustle and bustle in the corridor outside. Alan, the office manager, is rushing past the doorway and he's dragging Melanie along with him. His hand is tightly gripping her elbow and she's struggling to pull it free. Her face is twisted and I think he's hurting her. He's hurting Melanie. He's forcing her to go with him and she doesn't want to go. I must help her. She's going to be my girlfriend so I must help her. I put my cup on the desk and run out of the door into the corridor, but they are nowhere to be seen. Where have they gone, I wonder? I run along the corridor until I hear raised voices coming from the stationery cupboard. I push the door hard and it flies open.

"What the hell!" Alan shouts.

I grab his shoulder and pull him out of the cupboard.

"Leave her alone," I say. "Don't you dare hurt Melanie."

Alan's face is as white as a sheet and he looks angry and scared at the same time.

"You've got it wrong, Billy. I'm not hurting her we're just having a private talk. Isn't that right Melanie?"

I'm still gripping Alan's shoulder as I turn to look at Melanie.

"It's all right Billy, we were having a talk, but I'm going back to the typing pool now. You can let Alan go, he won't hurt me."

"But I saw him pulling your arm," I protest.

Melanie smiles and looks at Alan. It's a strange smile as if she's not really happy but pleased all the same.

"Thank you for caring about me Billy. Everything is all right now. Please go back to the dispatch room. I'm fine. Really I am."

I release Alan's shoulder and he immediately starts to rub it. Melanie walks past us and makes her way down the corridor, straightening her skirt as she goes.

"Well, what are you waiting for?" Alan says. "Get back to work. The show's over."

I walk slowly back to the dispatch room.

"Where did you get to?" Betty questions. "Your deliveries are ready to go. I've put them in alphabetical order beginning at 'Allendale.' There are only four calls, Billy, and they're all in or near Bath Street."

I stare hard at Betty. A is for Allendale. A is for Alan. Alan wrote the letter to Melanie. Alan was pulling Melanie and hurting her. Alan might be making trouble. It is Alan's letter I flushed down the toilet.

"Billy. Billy. Wake up. You are a dreamy Daniel today!"

Betty's voice interrupts my thoughts. I reach out and take my briefcase from her hands then walk into the corridor. The heavy glass outer door closes at my back before I remember I didn't say goodbye, but she'll understand, she's nice, besides I have other, more important things on my mind.

When I return to the office at lunchtime, I'm relieved to see that Mr. Henderson's car is safely back in its usual parking place. He must have got the 'trouble' sorted out. I walk straight to the typing pool because I want to check that Melanie is OK. Most of the girls are already away for lunch but Melanie is still at her desk. A man is sitting on the edge of her desk and I immediately feel worried, but as I get near, I'm relieved to see it isn't Alan. I walk closer for a better look and see that it's James Bond, the boy in the blazer. He's sitting on Melanie's desk and they're talking and laughing. After a moment, Melanie notices me and she stops talking. The boy turns around to face me.

"Hello," he says. "It's Billy, isn't it?"

"Y y yes," I stammer, suddenly unsure of myself.

What's he doing here I wonder? The boy stands and faces me.

"Allow me to formally introduce myself," he says extending his hand. "I'm Jez, sometimes known as James Bond."

Melanie giggles. I shake his hand.

"I'm Billy. Sometimes known as fuckwit," I respond, joining in the joke.

The boy punches my arm playfully.

"You're all right Billy," he says, and I smile at him.

"Well I'm going to lunch now," Melanie says, standing.

"Mind if I join you?" Jez asks. "I'm not very popular with my uncle at the moment. So it would suit me to get out of the old bastard's face. That's if you don't mind lunching with a younger man," he quips.

"I don't mind at all, as long as the younger man comes fully equipped," Melanie replies, with a leer.

Jez pulls a twenty-pound note from his blazer pocket.

"Oh, I'm always fully equipped," he answers smiling.

They both laugh, but I don't understand the joke. I stand watching them, not knowing what to say. They leave without saying goodbye.

CHAPTER TWELVE

MELANIE

Wow! Mr. Henderson's nephew might be young but there's no way you could call him a boy. He is drop dead gorgeous. He's at least six feet tall, lean and rangy with jet black hair and the brightest violet-coloured eyes I've ever seen. What a turn on. As we walk along the street Jez takes my hand, his touch is electric. I feel wet with excitement.

"Are you hungry?" I ask, trying to calm myself down.

"Only for you," he replies, squeezing my hand.

When we reach the corner of the street, Jez stops and he turns me towards him, his hands slide smoothly up my legs.

"I really want you," I gasp. "Where can we go?"

Jez says nothing but takes my hand again and leads me down a narrow side street. We're walking past tall, sandstone, Victorian terraces most of which are now turned into apartments for students. Suddenly Jez pulls me into the open doorway of a close.

"This will do," he says. "This will do for a bitch on heat."

He has a strange look in his eyes as he pushes me down onto the cold, stone stair. Within seconds he rolls my skirt up around my waist, opens my legs and roughly pushes himself into me. He tears at my blouse, yanks down my bra then fixes his mouth on my breasts, sucking and biting first one nipple then the other. I'm being pushed against the cold, hard stair and he's biting me and hurting me. His eyes are full of anger. He's frightening me and I want him to stop.

"Stop Jez, please stop," I beg. "You're hurting me."

I try to push him off, but the more I fight him the rougher he becomes. My struggling is turning him on and I'm scared now, he could really hurt me.

"Get off me Jez or I'll tell your uncle," I threaten.

As soon as the words are out of my mouth I know I've made a terrible mistake. His face twists with anger and he slaps my cheek. His thighs pound against me with renewed fury and I think I might be sick. Eventually I feel him climax inside me and he roughly pulls out of me and stands up. Through tear-filled eyes I watch him zip his trousers then he takes the twenty pound note from his pocket and throws it at me.

"That was good Melanie, really good." He leans over me and pushes his face close to mine.

"Don't worry, I'll be back for more and when I want you, I'll call you and expect you to come to me. Don't make me fetch you or I'll get angry and I might have to hurt you."

He stares into my eyes, his gaze is menacing.

"You do understand Melanie, don't you? You'll do whatever I want, whenever I want. If I tell you to fuck with a dog, you'll say, ' Yes Jez, Alsatian or Terrier?' because if you don't, I'll hurt you so badly that nobody will ever want you again. Do I make myself clear?"

I nod my head, I'd agree to anything right now just to get away from him.

"Good" he says and glances at his watch. "You'd better get a move on or you'll be late for work. My uncle hates it when people keep him waiting."

Jez straightens his clothes, slaps the dust from his trousers then turns and leaves. He's acting as if nothing has happened. I sit on the stair, bitten, bruised and covered in grime. How could he do that to me? I thought he liked me.

When I'm sure he's gone I struggle to my feet and clean myself up as best as I can with paper tissues. I feel dirty and degraded. No man has ever treated me like that. I hurry back to the office and manage to sneak into the ladies toilets before the lunch break is over, then I quickly wash my hands and face and wipe my legs with wet paper towels. My hands are shaking and I feel dazed. As I gaze at my reflection in the mirror, I struggle not to cry. He raped me. Jez raped me. Why? He knew I wanted him. He didn't need to hurt me or force me. Why? Why? Why? I stare hard at my face, my cheek is sore where Jez slapped me but fortunately there doesn't seem to be a mark. Carefully I re-apply my make-up and gradually a more familiar face appears in the mirror before me. I begin to feel angry. How dare he treat me like that, how dare he rape me? Who the hell does he think he is? And to make matters worse, to throw money at me as if I'm some kind of cheap prostitute. I check my face one last time before I go out to meet the world, my eyes stare back at me from the mirror, vulnerable and afraid. The memory of Jez's callous violence comes flooding back to me and my fear of him remains sharp and tangible. Yet somehow, I still want him. Somehow, I'm drawn to him. I want to possess him, frighten him and control him the way he controlled me.

CHAPTER THIRTEEN

JEZ

Bitch! Slag! She'll keep her knickers on now, fucking slag. Thought she'd fuck with me. Fuck my body. Fuck my brain. Fuck my wallet. Fuck the boss's nephew. See what she could get. She'll not be so quick to take her knickers off now. That poor sod Billy fancies her like mad, can't keep his eyes off her. He might have a lame brain but I bet he doesn't have a limp dick. Maybe I'll make her let Billy fuck her and give him a treat. That'll teach her to try and use me. Thought a schoolboy would be easy meat, not a chance, not a chance, bitch. I bet she's screwing half the men in that office. Maybe she's screwing Uncle Peter. Peter Henderson LLB. Limp, little bastard, hah, that's a good one. I must tell him that one. He'll have a stroke, silly, self-righteous sod. I wish the old bastard would die and leave me all his money. He's probably on his way to my school right now, full of indignation because I left his stinking office without telling him. He'll probably talk to that sad old poofter, David Goldman. Well I don't care. What can he do? Nothing. I don't give a monkey's fart.

CHAPTER FOURTEEN

BILLY

As I leave the typing pool, I practically bump into Mr. Henderson.

"Hello Billy," he says. "Have you seen my nephew? He should be around here somewhere. I told him to wait for me."

"If you mean Jez, he just went out to lunch with Melanie, but don't worry, he had money with him, he showed me."

"Jez. Jez." he spits out the words. "Hmph, I might have guessed that he'd call himself something like that. His name is Jeremy. That's the name he was christened. I suppose he thinks Jez is trendier."

I purse my lips, holding them tightly shut because I don't know if I'm meant to answer.

"That boy is going to land himself in serious trouble if he doesn't improve his attitude. He is always hanging around with the wrong sort of people. My sister's house is in a terrible state after his party and the housekeeper is distraught. I just don't know what to do with the boy."

I stare at the floor. Mr. Henderson is very upset and I feel embarrassed.

"If somebody doesn't keep a close eye on that boy he'll end up in jail, or worse, maybe dead."

My head jerks up, dead, James Bond, dead. I like Jez. He's kind to me. I don't want him to die.

"Keep an eye out for him, Billy. Will you please? Let me know if you see him."

My chest swells with pride. Mr. Henderson wants me to be the one to keep a close eye on Jez. He thinks I'm the person who can save him.

"I'll watch out for him, Mr. Henderson. Don't worry. Betty always says I don't miss much."

"Thank you, Billy," he replies, and smiles at me. "You are invaluable."

After Mr. Henderson leaves, I begin to work out a plan. I know where Jez goes to school and I know that he catches the bus at my stop. I could follow him, see where he lives then I'd be able to watch him. He'd never know. I could watch him and keep him safe and he'd never know. Then I'll be a spy just like James Bond. If only I'd spoken to Mr. Henderson earlier. If only I'd known. I could have followed Jez and Melanie when they went out to lunch. Mind you, I don't suppose he's in any danger from Melanie, she's not the 'wrong sort', she's beautiful. Besides, Jez will keep Melanie safe from Alan. Goodness, how busy I'm going to be, looking out for Melanie and Jez. No wonder Mr. Henderson thinks I'm invaluable.

When I arrive home for dinner, I begin to tell Mum all about my day.

"I saved Melanie from Alan and I'll probably be saving Jez's life. Mr. Henderson says I'm invaluable."

"That's fine Billy," she says. "But remember what

I've told you. You are there to work, concentrate on that. You mustn't get too involved with the people you work with because they don't like it and it's not right."

"But Mum," I protest.

"No buts, Billy. Your dinner is on the table, eat it up while it's hot."

I decide to say nothing more to Mum because she simply has no idea how important my work is. She just doesn't understand. Instead I sit at the table, pick up my fork and mix up the mince, peas and mashed potato that are on my plate. This is my favourite dinner and when I mix it all together, the whole plateful tastes of the lovely meaty gravy.

"When you finish eating Billy, I need you to run a message for me," Mum says." Aunty Mabel has been feeling a bit under the weather and that horrible Mrs. Worthington, who she lives with, is going out for the evening. I've prepared a food flask with a portion of dinner. I'd like you to run it round to her. It'll only take you about an hour altogether and she'll be so happy to see you."

"But Mum," I protest. "Animal Hospital is on the telly tonight. I love that programme."

"Well then get a move on and you'll be home in time for it. Or you can watch it at Aunty Mabel's. She'll be glad of the company."

There's no point in arguing with Mum so I put the last forkful of food in my mouth and stare at my empty plate.

"If you can be ready to leave in ten minutes Billy, I'll give you money to buy an ice cream at the cafe."

I decide to skip my usual cup of tea and head for Aunty Mabel's house. It's only ten minutes walk from my home, in a street immediately opposite the cafe.

As I walk up the steep hill, I lick my ice cream and wonder what is actually wrong with Aunty Mabel. I hope it isn't rabies. They talk about rabies on Animal Hospital and it sounds horrible. I decide to finish my ice cream before I go to see her, in case she coughs or sneezes on it. When Aunty Mabel opens the door, I stare hard at her. She's wearing a dressing gown and her face is very white.

"Have you got rabies?" I ask.

"No, my pet," she answers, smiling, "Just a cold. In you come, Billy."

I gaze around as I enter the hallway. I've never been to this house before. That is to say, I've never been inside. The hallway is very dark. Everything is wood, dark brown wood and it smells of polish. We enter the sitting room through a door at the end of the hall and a blast of hot air from the gas fire hits my face.

"This is a nice surprise, Billy," Aunty Mabel says.

"I've brought your dinner. It's in here," I say, handing her the food flask. "Can you turn on the telly please, Animal Hospital is coming on?"

"How kind of your Mum to think of me. This cold is very tiring and I really didn't feel up to cooking. Switch the television on, you may watch whatever you want."

I walk towards the telly and reach for the switch. Suddenly, I'm stopped in my tracks. There, frowning at me from the top of the telly, is a photo of the lady soldier. She's in her uniform and is wearing her blue hat.

"Who's this, Aunty Mabel?" I blurt out.

"Oh that. That's Bella Worthington. She's the lady I live with and I am afraid she looks exactly like her photograph. She's rather unpleasant, Billy, although I'm sure she doesn't mean to be. I live here as her companion and housekeeper. I have no choice, you see. I have nowhere else to go."

Aunty Mabel looks sad and I feel sorry for her.

"I have to watch the old dragon constantly or she'd make my life an absolute misery. She's a terrible bully, you see."

Poor Aunty Mabel, I think. It must be bad enough having to keep house for Mrs. Worthington and having to live with her, but to have to watch her as well. Ugh, what a scary thought.

"Don't worry Aunty Mabel," I say. "I'll watch her for you. You just get better. I'll watch her all the time and tell you everything she does. You don't have to bother about her anymore. I'll look after you."

"You're such a kind boy, Billy," she replies, reaching for her purse. "You get off home now, Pet, and buy yourself a sweetie on the way. Here's a pound. If you leave right away, you'll be home in plenty of time for your programme."

"Thanks Aunty Mabel," I say, taking the money and kissing her cheek. "Remember, don't you worry about Mrs. Worthington. I'll watch her for you. It will be easy for me now that I know who she is. I won't let her bully you anymore."

CHAPTER FIFTEEN

BELLA

It's lucky I came home early or I would never have known about that creature being in my house.

"Whatever were you thinking about, Mabel? What on earth made you invite that retarded man into my home? He might have broken one of my valuable antiques, or he might have turned violent and hurt you. Whatever possessed you?"

"In the first place," Mabel replies. "He is not violent. Neither is he destructive. He is my best friend's son and I have often spoken of him. His name is Billy. You know that I've mentioned him."

"Billy. Billy," I say, my voice rising. "You said Billy was a retarded boy. That hulking, great creature is a man. What was he doing here, in my house?"

Mabel sighs as if answering is a great effort.

"I am ill, Bella," she says. "I have a dreadful cold and I'm exhausted, but you probably didn't notice because you were in such a hurry to go out. Billy brought me some dinner my friend prepared for me."

"Are you implying that I don't care about you?"

"No, of course not," Mabel replies.

"I don't suppose I have to remind you that without

me you wouldn't have a roof over your head or food in your mouth."

"No Bella," Mabel says. "You don't need to remind me because you're constantly telling me."

"I'll pretend I didn't hear that remark because I know you're ill. People say funny things when they're ill. Things they don't really mean and might regret later."

Mabel sighs again. "I'm very tired, Bella. I think I'll go up to bed now."

"Aren't you going to make some tea first?" I ask. "I've been chairing meetings all evening and my throat is as dry as dust."

Mabel stares at me with her stupid, sheep dog eyes. She is so pathetic-looking and she irritates me.

"Oh go to bed, Mabel. I'll make my own tea," I snap, then I head for the kitchen.

I hear her footsteps on the stairs and I'm relieved that I don't have to look at her pathetic, self-pitying face again. As I wait for the tea to brew, I think about the retarded man. I decide to take a closer look at him when I next see him on the bus. I don't like the idea of him being in my home, but I'll give him the benefit of the doubt. If he doesn't look violent, I might allow him to visit Mabel, with certain restrictions of course. Once I've had the opportunity for a closer inspection of him, I'll tackle Mabel regarding the house rules. After all, I am a Christian. I have Christian values and, however damaged he might be, I must not forget he is one of God's creatures.

CHAPTER SIXTEEN

BILLY

It's a special day today because my mum is having a tea party. She said if I'm a good boy and fetch the shopping and clean the house for her, she'd let me have a cake after dinner and money to go to the cinema.

"I don't want you here when my friends come round tonight," she says. "We're going to discuss what to do about that awful woman from number six. You know the one I mean, the drunken one with the delinquent daughter. Mrs. Grimes is sure she's the one stealing the washing off the clotheslines and I'm positive she stole my garden gnome. The discussion might get rather unpleasant. You'll be better off at the cinema," she continues. "Paul is on duty tonight. He's a nice man and he'll see that no one starts with you."

I love the cinema. Last time I was there to see a film about a spy. The cinema was quite quiet, apart from the girls who sat beside me. They said they knew me but I didn't remember knowing them. They asked me to buy them cigarettes and they gave me money to buy chocolate for myself. They were really nice girls and when they realised I was on my own, they sat beside me. They told me they were in fourth year at school.

"Exams this year, worst luck," Tricia said. "Worst luck," Emma agreed. "Fucking awful luck," Gill said. Then they all laughed. Gill and Emma sat on either side of me and Tricia sat next to Gill.

When Paul came round to check on me, he said, "Don't you think you should move along a bit, girls and leave Billy alone?" "We know him, Mister," Emma replied. "He lives near our Cathie. We're sitting here so nobody starts with him. We know he's not right."

"They're my friends, Paul," I added. "I know them. I'm alright."

"That's okay Billy," he said. "I'll see you after the show then."

When the lights went out, Gill leaned across me and whispered something to Emma then they all giggled. The next thing I knew Gill put her hand on my lap. She started to rub my private parts. It felt so good. I shut my eyes and imagined I was with Molly in her pink, fluffy bedroom. Then the music for the film began.

"Stop or I'll miss the film," I whispered. Gill giggled.

"Stop or I'll miss the film," she mimicked, but she didn't stop. I know what she was doing was wrong, but it felt so good that I didn't care and Mum never knew.

As usual Mum was driving me mad, giving me all these stupid jobs to do. At last I'm out of the house. At last I'm at the cinema. At last I'm in my usual seat. I take off my coat and roll it up then put it on the seat beside me. The weight of it holds the seat down. I've got my popcorn, my sweets and my drink arranged neatly on my coat. It's just like having a little table beside me.

"That's me all set," I say to the man in front. "Look everything's neat." The man nods but he doesn't turn round. He's not very friendly. I look around for someone I know but the girls aren't here this time. "I'm all set," I say again. This time the man moves. I'm quite pleased because his head was in the way and I like to sit in my usual seat.

When the movie finishes and I step outside and I see it's only 8.30 as I've been to the early showing. If I go home this early, Mum will be angry, but I can't see another film as I've spent all my money on sweets. I know, I'll go to the cemetery in Netherlee Road and watch the people walking their dogs. It's a very old cemetery with big trees and lots of bushes. It reminds me of a park.

I haven't walked very far when I see a man sitting on a wall. His head is resting on his hands and he doesn't look very well. I know him, I think to myself, he's James Bond's teacher. As I get nearer to him, I see he's being sick and I run to help him.

CHAPTER SEVENTEEN

DAVID

That bastard, when I think of all the times he told me he loved me, usually when I had his dick in my mouth. When I think of all I've done for him, all the contacts I made for him, now he says it's over. 'We have to move on,' he says. Well it isn't over for me, I love him. I love him. He didn't even have the decency to come to my house to tell me, after a year of doing everything for him. Everything. One drink at Napoleons and we're through. One drink and he delivers that fucking awful line. 'We must move on,' he says. And that's it, over, finished, finito, the end. I wonder whose cock he's sucking now? Which lucky bugger is going to be his next step on the social ladder?

God, I feel awful, so much gin so little time. Ha, I suppose I think I'm funny. I must sit down for a while. I'm too drunk to walk. I wish I was home. I'm right next to the cinema and the station is just round the corner, if I can just make it to the train. It's only about 8.30, it's not far to walk, surely I'll make the 8.45.

"Are you alright, Sir? Can I help you?"

Someone is blocking out the light.

"It's me, Billy. Do you need help?"

"Billy. Oh I remember you, sweet Billy boy. I'm not very well."

I stare into his bright blue eyes, his jaw hanging slack with concern. Then I look down at my vomit-splashed shoes and find myself blubbering like a child.

"I've had a fight with my friend, Billy. He doesn't love me anymore," I sob.

"Don't worry, Sir," Billy says trying to comfort me. "I'll be your friend. I'll look after you. Just tell me what to do to make you happy."

I feel a stirring in my loins as obscene thoughts meander through my drink-sodden brain.

"You can be my friend, Billy. You can make me happy. Have you got time to help me home?"

"Yes, I can help you, I don't have to be back until 11.30," he says, proudly.

I feel myself being hoisted off the wall and onto my feet as if I weighed no more than a child. I don't remember how we got to my rooms but I do remember Billy helping me out of my coat and taking my shoes to wash the vomit off them. I'm lying on my bed, watching Billy tidying up the debris from earlier. I can't help noticing his strong shoulders and firm buttocks as he moves about the room. My hand instinctively reaches for my crotch. I'm hovering between sleep and pleasure when Billy's voice shouts me back to consciousness.

"My Mum doesn't let me do that," He says. "She says it's a sin against God and nature and if I'm lucky not to go blind, God will still find a way to punish me."

"Your Mum's quite right," I answer. "But it's only really a sin if you do it to yourself. If you do it to someone else or if they do it to you, it's just massage and even doctors recommend that."

I stare into his confused, kind eyes and I start to cry. How can I stoop so low? How can I take advantage of a simple soul like Billy? I just can't seem to help myself. Great gasping sobs expel from my throat and I can't seem to get control of myself.

"I'm all alone again," I say, partly to Billy, partly to myself. "I'm so tired of being lonely."

Billy's huge muscular arm goes round my shoulder and he pulls my head to his chest and pats my hair.

"Don't be sad," he says. "I'll look after you. I'll be your friend."

I hesitate for a moment then I take Billy's other hand in mine and I hope I don't go blind as I encourage him to sin against God and nature.

CHAPTER EIGHTEEN

BILLY

Monday comes around once more and I don't care about Mum's list of jobs today as I have more important things to think about. I began my invaluable work on Saturday by following Melanie and I can see how she could easily get into trouble. On Saturday morning I took her mail from Frank the postman. I said I was going to visit her so he handed the letters to me. Of course, I took them home to check them first. One of the letters was just stuff about her mobile phone and it didn't seem to be important, but I copied her telephone number into my notebook, just in case I ever need to phone her and warn her of imminent danger. That's what superheroes call it. They say 'beware, imminent danger.' The other letter was very rude. It was from a man who called her terrible names and said he wasn't going to pay her any money. Melanie doesn't need his money, she has a great job and she certainly doesn't need to read the horrible words he wrote. I threw both of the letters in the bin so in the end, I didn't have to post anything through her letterbox.

I watched her house after dinner on Saturday as

well. She didn't know I was watching because I was hiding in her neighbour's garden behind their garden shed. I checked my 'Star Trek' watch and it was 7.35 exactly when a car drove up. Melanie got into the car with a stranger and let him kiss her. Everybody knows that you don't get into cars with strangers. She certainly wasn't making my job easy. I tried to run after the car to see where she was going, but it screeched away at high speed. The man was a terrible driver and I was worried they might crash.

On Sunday afternoon I watched her hanging her underwear on the clothesline. I was in my special hiding place. The underwear was shiny and lacy. It was the sort of stuff Molly would have worn in her bedroom. I think underwear like that should be seen only in private. What kind of impression does it give to the neighbours, putting shiny, lacy panties and brassieres on the line in full view of everyone? When Melanie went back indoors I ran into her garden and quickly took them off the line. Then I stuffed them into my briefcase, ran all the way to the main road and pushed them into the green, metal bin outside the chip shop. I knew the bin men would come on Monday morning and empty the bin into the crusher then nobody would ever know they were Melanie's.

It isn't an easy job, looking after Melanie, but somebody has to protect her. I will always stay hidden so she'll never know it's me looking after her. I'll be just like a superhero. Captain Invaluable, that's me.

CHAPTER NINETEEN

MELANIE

"Mother," I shout at the top of my voice. "Mum," I shout again.

"What is your problem?" my mother yells back.

"Where have you put my 'Diva' undies? I put three sets on the line and now they've gone, but they're not in my drawer."

"I haven't touched them," my mother replies. "I've told you time and time again you have to look after your own things."

"Well I haven't got them," I say, indignantly. "If you don't have them then some pervert's probably stolen them off the line."

"Perhaps one of your boyfriends took them as a memento," my mother says, spitefully. "I've told you before to dress more sensibly. You always give the wrong impression. One day it will get you into real trouble."

"I'd rather have a bit of excitement in my life than be dead like you," I mutter to myself.

I'm about to rush out of the door when I realise there's no mail on the hall table.

"Mum," I say. "I was expecting a letter from a

friend and the bill for my mobile. You haven't taken them in, have you?"

"You know all the mail gets left on the hall table," she replies. "If it's not there then it hasn't come."

As if on cue, my mobile phone begins to ring. I'm already late and don't really have time for this.

"Hello," I snap into the phone. "Who is this?" There's silence. "Who is this?" I demand again.

"Don't worry," a male voice says. "I'm watching you."

The call ends abruptly. How strange I think to myself, it must have been a wrong number, but a jag of fear lingers. I dial 1471, only to find that the caller's number is withheld.

I grab my coat and bag and head off towards the main road. The sky is grey and I wonder why it always seems to start raining the second I step out of the house. As I approach the bus stop, I see Billy McDaid waiting there. What on earth is he doing here? I wonder. This isn't his stop. This is all I need on a miserable Monday morning. There will be no avoiding him and he'll insist on showing me what's in his damned briefcase.

The bus arrives at the stop the same time as me and Billy stands aside to let me on first. I quickly sit down beside an elderly lady. Not my first choice of travelling companion as I usually prefer to find a good-looking young man, but beggars can't be choosers and it's better than sitting next to Billy all the way into town. There's some chopping and changing of seats as people arrange to sit next to their friends and Billy manages to place himself on the seat directly behind me.

As the journey progresses, I'm lost in my

thoughts, wondering what could have happened to the money I was expecting from Alan. Maybe he's calling my bluff or maybe he found the courage to tell his wife about us after all. This abortion scam only works if I can get him to pay up. Maybe the mail is simply late and it will be waiting for me when I get home from work.

I am dragged from my thoughts by the sound of laughter. Everybody is looking out of the windows and giggling. The bus is stopped at the school crossing and, as I take a look out of the window, I can see what's causing the amusement. Three little boys are dancing about as they cross from the shops to the school. They are wiggling their hips and sashaying and swaying as they sing the words to the song "sex bomb" at the tops of their voices. Each has a pair of knickers on his head and a bra stuffed with what seems to be old chip papers round his chest.

"Look at them," says the lady beside me. "Aren't they a scream?"

I am about to agree when suddenly, I recognise the bras and panties. They are my 'Diva' undies, the ones that disappeared from the clothesline on Saturday. I feel my face flush. I'm mortified. How on earth did these horrible little boys get hold of them, I wonder? They cost me a fortune, nearly a week's wages, but I can hardly reclaim them now. I'm aware of hot breath on the back of my neck and turn round quickly to see Billy. His face is as red as my face feels.

CHAPTER TWENTY

BILLY

I watch the boys as I stare out of the bus window and wonder why the bin lorry is so late today. Melanie's underwear should have been in the crusher before the boys could find it. I can't help thinking about what she would look like in the silky, lacy panties. I feel my face go red and I get that special tickly feeling in my lap and I can't help touching myself there. I am leaning forward and I can smell Melanie's hair. Suddenly she turns round to face me and her face is as red as a beetroot. She should be really grateful that I'm the only one who knows they were her bras and panties. I'm still rubbing myself when the man sitting beside me gives me a dirty look and hisses, "Stop that", loudly in my ear. I sit up with a start. Mum would be really angry with me. I try to think about the film I saw at the weekend to take my mind off my dirty thoughts.

When I get into work Betty says my deliveries aren't quite ready. So she makes me a cup of tea with two sugars and gives me a chocolate biscuit. Betty is so kind. Sometimes I wish she was my Mum. As I drink my tea and eat my biscuit, she tells me it will be her birthday on Wednesday and that she'll be sixty.

"You mustn't tell anyone my age, Billy," she says. "It'll be our secret. A lady never likes people to know how old she is."

I decide to go to the shops at lunchtime and buy Betty a present. I think I'll buy a nice tin of biscuits from Marks and Spencer's. Mum always says that a tin of biscuits from Marks and Spencer's is an appropriate gift for most occasions. I've got my ten pounds of emergency money in my zipped-up, inside pocket. I'll use that and explain it to Mum when I get home. I just hope there isn't an emergency.

Once I get started, the morning passes quite quickly. I have only four deliveries to make and they are all near to each other in the city centre. At lunchtime I make my way along Argyle Street towards Marks and Spencer. As I enter the shop, I see Jez at the door. He's standing just inside the shop and is looking all around as if he's watching and waiting for someone. I'm walking towards him when I notice the bad boys who frightened me at the court house. They're quite near to Jez and I can see the boys taking clothes off the rail and putting them into a big bag. They're going to steal the clothes. I'm sure they're here to steal things from Mr. Marks and Spencer's. I must tell my friend Jez. He'll know what to do. He'll stop the bad boys. They're frightened of him because he's like James Bond.

I run towards him and shout, "Help, help, James Bond, help, help. The bad boys are here."

Jez turns to me and his face goes white. "Shut up, Billy," he hisses, "Stop shouting."

"But the bad boys are here. They're stealing things," I say.

The bad boys run towards the door and two men in uniforms are running after them. They all run through the door and the alarm bells go off. The shop policemen manage to catch two of the boys but the third boy gets away. It's very exciting. I turn to talk to Jez but he's gone. I suppose he's late for school and I have to leave too or I'll be late.

As the shop policemen march the boys back inside the shop, one of the boys calls out to me. "We'll get you for this, moron. You're dead meat." As he's dragged past, he spits at me, but the spit misses me and lands instead on some clothes hanging on a rail.

"Disgusting," A lady who's standing beside me says. "Well done, Dear," she says to me, "Well done."

I feel very proud because I stopped a robbery. I race back to the office to tell everyone and completely forget to buy Betty's present.

CHAPTER TWENTY-ONE

JEZ

Shit! Shit! Shit! Derek and Tony lifted for thieving, stupid, stupid, idiots. Why did they run out of the shop? It wasn't theft until they left with the stuff. How could they be so stupid? How on earth will I get my jellies now without the clothes to exchange? And without the jellies I won't get the money for my investment. Shit, shit, shit how could they be so stupid?

Well that's it, everything's up in the air now. They will be jailed. No warnings this time, they will go down. Why did Billy have to come into the shop? Why did he have to make so much bloody noise? If he hadn't drawn attention to us, I would be five hundred quid better off. To make matters worse, he raced back to my uncle's office and blabbed to everyone. Now that Uncle Limpdick knows I was there, I'll never hear the end of it.

I wouldn't like to be in Billy's shoes when Derek and Tony get out. They'll be livid and I won't be able to help him because they'll probably be mad at me too. Some look-out I turned out to be. If that idiot

Billy hadn't shouted to me, they'd have been home and dry and I'd be counting my money now.

Christ it's nearly six o'clock I'd better move it. I've to meet the great man himself at six-thirty. Summoned like some servant to Uncle, the Great Man, Henderson for dinner at the Great House. He thinks my 'waywardness', as he calls it, stems from a lack of family values. He blames it on the breakdown of family life. What a load of shite. Every child of rich parents has the confidence to go out into the world and succeed. I wouldn't expect my parents to give up on their lives to mollycoddle me. Does he expect them to stay at home with me? I can just see us all, sitting in front of the telly, playing Monopoly. He just hasn't got a clue. Now I've to go through the motions and appease the old bastard. We are to have dinner together once a week and I've to tell him what I have planned for the week ahead and discuss anything that's bothering me. If I don't do this, he says, he'll see to it that Mater and Pater send me off to some fucking boarding school while they're out travelling the world. He says he won't take responsibility for me otherwise. I might as well be inside with Derek and Tony and it's all, that idiot, Billy's fault. What am I going to tell him? 'Well uncle, this week I made £300 selling drugs, £150 from stolen cigarettes and £50 from prostitution,' that should go down like a ton of bricks.

I arrive at Uncle's promptly at six-thirty, wearing my best suit and clutching a bottle of ' Châteauneuf-du-Pape', lifted from a wedding I gate-crashed at the Hilton.

I'm handed a sickly-sweet sherry as an aperitif then ushered into the dining room. We sit at either end of a table designed for eight and it's immediately apparent that the generation gap is as wide as the table. I don't want to make it easy for my uncle because I feel I've been blackmailed to attend. I manage to reply with single word answers to questions regarding my schoolwork, my teachers and my friends.

He makes a frantic last-ditch attempt at conversation and asks me if I have a girlfriend. I can't resist shocking the old bastard by saying, "Actually uncle, I'm very unsure about my sexuality, but I think having a gay teacher has taught me a lot about relationships. I think it's wonderful that the school board have no prejudices."

His face goes red and, for a moment, I think I've gone too far. After all I don't want to give him a stroke or I will be shipped off to boarding school. I don't know if his high colour is from shock or anger, shock at my dubious sexuality or anger that a poof is teaching at a £5000 a term school.

CHAPTER TWENTY-TWO

BILLY

I've had such an exciting day, everyone at work thinks I'm a hero. Mr. Henderson was particularly interested to hear about Jez being at the shops too. I can't wait to get home to tell my mum. I know I'm not meant to talk to strangers but I can't stop myself telling the people on the bus. As a reward, Mr. Henderson has let me leave an hour early so the bus is quite quiet. Most of the regular people weren't at the stop, only the lady soldier got on with me. I've told four people about the bad boys and they were all very impressed. The only person I haven't told is the lady soldier, but I think she must have heard about it when I told the lady sitting beside her.

I find the lady soldier very scary, but I promised Aunty Mabel I'd keep an eye on her. I sat on the wall outside her house for a while on Sunday, just in case Aunty Mabel needed me. I got tired after a while and there didn't seem to be anyone around, so I just went home.

I think I'll get off the bus at the lady soldier's stop then, when she rings the bell to get in, I can call out to Aunty Mabel and tell her about my exciting day.

She'll be so proud of me and she might give me money for sweets as a reward.

Betty, at work, says I should get a reward. She thinks Mr. Marks and Spencer should give me something for saving him from the robbers. I wonder if he'll give me a medal. Then I remember that superheroes don't get rewards, they just get to feel good for doing good deeds.

CHAPTER TWENTY-THREE

BELLA

I hate travelling by bus, particularly when it's full of poor, smelly people. I don't think the poor buy enough soap and yet they always seem to be able to afford cigarettes. That's why they smell so bad. It never ceases to amaze me when smokers don't know how badly they smell.

On top of the discomfort, I have to suffer that infernal retarded man's ramblings. He's told the same ridiculous story to every person on the bus. However, for some reason he's decided not to force himself upon me. He must realise I'm above such nonsense.

I'm absolutely exhausted after the shambles of the old soldiers' day out. Despite all the planning and meticulous arrangements to take them for an afternoon of singing and music, the coach company sent us the wrong driver. I knew something was wrong and I told him so.

"Oh no," he assured me, "Don't you worry, Hen," he said. "I know the way."

He did indeed know the way, but not to where we were going. Instead we ended up at Scotland's biggest theme park. How could they mix us up with the scouts?

Grace said we really should try to make the best of it as it was too late to go anywhere else and for once I had to agree. I didn't, in my wildest dreams, expect her to put three incontinent old men onto the 'waltzer'. I only left them for a few minutes to visit the lavatory. I should have stuck to them like glue. I can't imagine how the attendant managed to get the seats clean. Then to let Charlie go on the aeroplane ride when he was already shell-shocked from being shot down over France. How could she be so stupid? And I don't know what she was thinking about when she bought them all hotdogs. Three of them were sick on the way home, although that was partly due to the driver thinking he was in a formula one race. What a day, what a terrible, ghastly day.

I'm also rather worried by a conversation I had recently with Agnes from the Bearsden branch of the Women's Institute. She told me she pays her companion, Annie, £100 a week together with free room and board and she said that's the going rate. I pay Mabel £60 a week and I make her pay a share of the Council Tax and telephone bill. I've been thinking about this for some time and I've decided to tell Mabel I'll leave her my house when I die. She's always going on about not having anywhere to go. By telling her that, she'll stay with me to make sure she doesn't miss out on an inheritance and she'll be too frightened to ask for a pay rise, but there's no need to change my will just yet. After all, who knows what the future will bring?

I feel the idiot's eyes upon me and I wonder why

he's even on this bus. I'm about an hour earlier today so he must be early too. He seems to always be around these days and I don't like it. I don't like it one little bit. Mabel encourages him far too much. I don't panic easily and I'm certainly not prone to vivid imaginings, but I'm sure I saw him hanging around on Sunday. I didn't want him to see me looking at him so I hid behind the net curtains, but he was definitely outside the house. He frightens me somewhat. I'm sure these people can sometimes turn violent. Mabel wasn't even home as she was doing my hospital sick visiting for me because I was feeling rather tired.

At last I'm at my stop. As I step down from the bus the retarded man jumps off practically landing on me. I set off at a quick march and he falls into step behind me. He is nearly walking up my heels. I feel threatened by him. There is no need for him to get off at this stop and certainly no need for him to walk so close to me. I spin round and confront him.

"Why are you following me?" I shout. "Get away from me. Be off with you."

He stares at me with those empty eyes then runs away towards Stamperland.

I feel quite unnerved by the experience and race into my house. I simply must speak to Mabel about him because I no longer feel safe in my own home, and I can't have that. I simply can't have that.

CHAPTER TWENTY-FOUR

BILLY

My mother is waiting for me when I come down for breakfast. She has a serious look on her face and I wonder if I've done something wrong.

"Sit down, Billy," she says. "I want to talk to you."

I'm sure something is wrong as she's never this serious.

"Have you been to visit Aunty Mabel's house recently?" she asks.

I try to think of the right answer. Does she want me to say yes, or no? Have I forgotten something important?

"Billy," Mum says raising her voice. "I asked you a question."

I stare at the floor. I must give an answer or she'll get really angry.

"I got off the bus at her stop yesterday," I say. "I wanted to tell her about saving Mr. Marks and Spencer from the robbers. The lady soldier got off the bus and she shouted at me. I got a fright and ran home. I didn't see Aunty Mabel. I didn't even go through the gate."

"Is that the whole truth, Billy? You're not missing anything out?" she asks.

I shake my head. "I'm not leaving anything out, Mum. Cross my heart and hope to die."

"Okay, Billy," she says. "Eat your breakfast and we'll say no more about it."

I'm worried about what has happened. Has the lady soldier said something bad about me? Maybe she doesn't want me to keep an eye on her. Maybe she wants to upset Aunty Mabel and she can't if I'm watching her. I think I'd better keep a very close eye on her, even if she does scare me. Nobody is going to hurt my aunty. Not while I'm around.

When I get into work, I'm pleased to see I have a delivery for the school because I'll be able to visit David. He said that, as we are friends now, I may call him David, instead of 'Sir'. Maybe he'll want me to visit him tonight after work to stop him from being lonely. He's so kind to me and I like it when he calls me 'his sweet Billy boy'.

Maybe I'll see Jez and then I'll be able to report back to Mr. Henderson. He was really pleased when I told him Jez was at Marks and Spencer. He said it was about time someone knew what that boy was up to.

When I arrive at the school, I see David at the entrance and I run up to speak to him.

CHAPTER TWENTY-FIVE

DAVID

I'm sitting in the Rector's office waiting for God, as we affectionately call him, to arrive. I have no idea why I've been summoned, but when God calls you, you must obey. His opulent office reminds me of a film set. It encompasses everything the archetypal Rector should have, from the dark oak panelling on the walls to the rich mahogany and green, leather furniture. The room smells of a mixture of leather polish and the acrid, slightly burning aroma of the electric bar fire. There is a phrenology head sitting on top of the bookcase behind the desk and a very un-p.c. stuffed owl on the bureau.

I would like to take off my jacket as the room is stuffy and too warm, but I know if I do, it would be considered presumptuous of me. So I sit, waiting, sweating slightly and occupying myself by reading the spines of the books in the bookcase and I wish he would get a move on. Time always seems to pass slowly when you're uncomfortable and this is no exception.

After about ten minutes, which feels like an hour to me, God makes his entrance. On first impressions you could be mistaken into thinking of him as a kindly, grandfatherly sort of chap, but as the Chinese people in their wisdom warn, beware the smiling devil.

"Sorry for keeping you waiting, David," he says. It's a throw-away line lacking any sincerity.

"Not at all," I reply, equally insincere.

"Would you like tea?" he inquires.

I know something is seriously amiss. God never offers tea to a teacher. It is a pleasure reserved for paying guests, namely the parents or guardians of the privileged monsters in our care.

"No thank you, Sir, I've just had a cup," I lie.

"Well we had better get right down to business," he says, shifting uncomfortably in his chair. "I have had an enquiry from a concerned guardian. It may involve your private life I'm afraid," he begins. "The gentleman is asking for my assurance about the moral tone of your teaching. How can I put it?" He hesitates, searching for the right words. "He wishes assurance that your moral tone will not influence your pupils' adversely. Do you understand what I'm saying David?" he asks.

"Not really, Sir," I reply. However, at the mention of a concern about my private life, I feel I know where this conversation is going.

"Do I need to spell it out, David?" he says, annoyance creeping into his voice.

"Yes Sir, I'm afraid you do," I reply.

"You're not making this easy, David," he says, his smile turning into a grimace.

Damn right I'm not, I think to myself. My integrity is being questioned. He fingers his collar nervously. I'm sweating buckets.

"The bottom line is," he begins. "I received a phone call from a gentleman who is an 'old boy' of this school. He is concerned that his nephew may be being influenced by your homosexuality. He thinks the boy is confused about his own sexuality. I have to know whether you have had any contact with your pupils outside of the classroom and whether the content of your lessons could, in any way, be perceived as controversial. This is a very serious matter."

I am instantly outraged. "This is nonsense," I splutter. "Utter nonsense. Who has said this about me? Who is making these false accusations? I never have any contact with pupils outside of the school and I certainly do not discuss my private life with them inside or outside of the classroom."

"Sit down, David," the Rector says. "Calm yourself."

I'm so angry that I'm not even aware of having stood up. I'm about to demand he tells me who's making the accusations, when it suddenly dawns on me, an 'old boy' of the school who is the guardian of a nephew. It must be Jez's uncle, Mr. Henderson. It all fits. Jez has been teasing me and tormenting me for weeks and, although I have never given any indication to the boy, or to anyone else for that matter, I do find every aspect of him irresistible, even his cruelty excites me. I slump back into my chair. Although I'm innocent of the accusations, I feel defeated.

"That's much better. Stay seated please, we must discuss this calmly. I assured the gentleman his fears would be groundless. However, it is my duty to investigate such a matter and that is why this conversation is necessary. The gentleman did indicate the boy has been troubled lately, due to a lack of parental input, and he might contrive something to gain attention."

That's not it, I think. That's not it at all. He is just a cruel, conniving, little bastard. I feel totally drained and exhausted.

"Well David," he continues. "As far as I'm concerned, the matter is closed. That's the lunchtime bell. I'll walk you to the door."

I manage to drag myself out of the chair and we exit the stifling room and make for the main entrance door. As I stand in the doorway with him, I fear I might burst into tears. I feel so vulnerable and struggle to compose myself. Then horror of horrors, I hear my name being called in the sing-song voice a child uses when he is excited.

"David. Oh David. It's me, your sweet Billy boy."

God and I turn simultaneously in the direction of the voice and I don't know who is more horrified, as Billy gallops up with his arms open wide and embraces me in a bear hug.

CHAPTER TWENTY-SIX

BILLY

David pats me on the back. "My, my, Billy," he says. "You are excited today." Then he turns to the man who's standing next to him and says, "You can see how it is with Billy, Sir. He's a special person. I've known the family for years, hence the familiarity." I didn't realise David knew my family but it doesn't matter. I care only that we are friends.

"Will I come round to your house tonight?" I ask. "We can watch telly and eat popcorn and put out the lights and pretend we're in the cinema."

The man who's standing next to David says, "I'll leave you now David, as I must get on. Please move away from the doorway," he adds. "In view of our previous conversation, I don't want anyone to get the wrong impression."

As David and I walk into the playground he asks, "When we are pretending to be at the cinema will you give me a massage?"

I don't really like giving the massage because I'm still not sure it's okay, but David is my best friend and I want to make him happy. I don't say anything to him, but I nod my head to say yes.

"That's great Billy," he says. "I'll hire a DVD shall I, how about 'Goldfinger'?"

"That will be great," I reply. "I love James Bond films."

"Hello there, Billy. Hello Sir." I turn to see Jez standing behind us. "Arranging some private tuition, Billy?" he asks. "Perhaps a bit of extra-curricular activity, Sir?"

"Hello Jez," I reply. "David is my friend and we are arranging our evening together. We're going to see a film and have popcorn," I tell him.

"Well isn't that cosy, are you going to sit in the back row?" he asks and licks his lips and winks at David.

"That's enough, Jez," David says. "Shouldn't you be in a class?"

"On my way, Sir," Jez replies. "Have fun Billy. Don't do anything I wouldn't do. That should leave you plenty of scope."

I think about what Jez has said and wonder if he would give David a massage. I decide he probably would if David was his best friend and if he got popcorn and to see a film.

"I'll see you later then, David," I say. "When should I come round?"

"About seven o'clock, Billy," he answers. "Oh, and Billy," he says. "Don't tell anyone about the massage. It's a private secret between you and me. Okay?"

"Okay," I reply. "And don't you tell anyone either."

I don't want my Mum to find out because I'm sure she wouldn't understand.

CHAPTER TWENTY-SEVEN

MELANIE

I'm really surprised not to have received anything from Alan yet. I'm sure I pressed all the right buttons when we last discussed my fake pregnancy. I simply must get him to pay up or I won't be able to afford my holiday.

I'm almost twenty minutes late arriving at the office because I just had to paint my nails before leaving home and I missed the bus. As I enter the typing pool, Alan is at the door.

"You're late, Melanie," he says, sternly.

"Well da-ha, Alan," I reply, expecting him to laugh.

"This is neither the time nor the place for frivolity," he says.

He is so serious, I feel a small jag of fear. This isn't the Alan I know and manipulate, the quiet, gentle soul who wouldn't say boo to a goose. Something has changed.

"Hurry up and get to your desk," he says, "Before you lose any more of the day. Take this as an official warning about your time-keeping and don't be late again."

Most of the girls sitting at their desks can hear what he's said and they're gossiping and giggling. How dare he speak to me like that in front of everyone. He might be the office manager, but I'm in control. Who the hell does he think he is?

"Melanie," Alan's voice booms out across the office. "Are you planning to do any work, or are you going to stand there all day?"

All eyes are upon me and I feel my face redden as I quickly take off my coat and sit down at my desk. Alan approaches my desk and whispers menacingly. "Things are going to change around here, my girl. You are on the way out. You cannot afford to be one minute late or get one thing wrong or I'll have you. You'll be out of here so quick your feet won't touch the ground. I hope you've taken on board everything I said in my letter, you scheming little bitch."

"What letter?" I ask." I didn't receive any letter."

Alan turns his back on me and walks away shaking his head. I feel sick to my stomach. He is obviously calling my bluff. What will I do now? I force myself to concentrate on my work. Until I can think of some way of handling this, I can't afford to make any mistakes. By lunchtime I have a blinding headache.

Alan hasn't come near me all morning. Instead, all my work has been passed to me by Geraldine, the office sneak.

"My, my, how the mighty fall," she says with a smirk, as she passes me a pile of copy typing. "No longer the favoured pet," she says. "What a shame, poor Melly. Why don't we feel sorry for you, I wonder?"

I don't answer her. I just keep my head down and try to ignore her, but my cheeks are burning.

At lunchtime everyone leaves the office except me. I sit at my desk and rest my aching head in my hands.

"Have you missed me?" a voice asks. "I'm sure you must have missed every throbbing inch of me."

I look up to see that Jez has parked himself on my desk. He's so stunningly handsome that he makes me gasp. His beauty is only equalled by his cruelty. He frightens me, particularly after our last encounter and yet I am drawn to him like a moth to a flame.

"Oh Jez," is all I can manage to say before bursting into tears. He places his arm gently round my shoulders as I sob.

"Don't cry, Melanie," he says. "We all have bad days. They don't last forever."

He produces a handkerchief and dabs at my tears. Am I seeing his gentle side, I wonder? Maybe he was just angry about something the last time we met. Maybe I came on too strong and gave him the wrong impression. Maybe he thought I'd be turned on by his roughness. It was probably all my fault.

"You are as strong and tough as I am," he continues. "That's what I like best about you. Something must be very wrong for you to be this upset."

I don't know what to say so I just nod and let him comfort me. Then he begins to speak again.

"I've recently lost two of my best friends," he says. "So I know what it's like to be hurt. Maybe you and I could hook up and console each other. It looks like we both have to find new beginnings. What do you say?"

"Thank you, Jez," I reply. "I'd like that."

He leans over and kisses me on the cheek. His lips are soft and gentle and he smells wonderful.

At that moment, Alan comes back into the office.

"What's going on here?" he demands. "You know you're not meant to be in here at lunchtime, Melanie. You can carry on this liaison with your boyfriend somewhere else."

I sense Jez stiffen with anger and he slowly turns to face Alan.

"Do you know who I am?" he asks, between gritted teeth.

Alan takes a step backwards. "Of course I know who you are," he replies, "Mr. Henderson's nephew."

"Oh, I'm much more than that," Jez says. "I'm his heir. One day this company will be mine. I'm being groomed to take over, so my Uncle can retire. I have a lot of influence over him. Melanie and I are friends and, if you want to continue working here, you'd better remember it."

Alan's face drains of colour. "Being Mr. Henderson's nephew doesn't give you the right to change the office rules," he says. "Don't force me to make an issue out of this." He's trying to be assertive but he's obviously not so sure of himself and, after a moment, he walks away.

"What just happened there?" I ask

"What happened is we won, Melanie. The fucker backed down. Come on Mel you can buy me lunch," he says, as he tucks my hand under his arm and marches me out of the door.

During the three o'clock tea break I'm summoned to Alan's room.

"Sit down, Melanie," he says, then he throws an envelope onto the desk in front of me.

"It's all there, six hundred pounds. Now you can get rid of the baby and leave me alone. You're a scheming little blackmailer. I can't believe you used Mr. Henderson's nephew to force me to pay. What's he getting out of this?"

I'm absolutely gobsmacked, he thinks I've used Jez. He actually thinks I was going to tell Mr. Henderson.

"Take your blood money and get back to work. Don't push me any further or you'll regret it," he adds.

I lift the envelope and leave his room.

"More trouble, Melanie?" Geraldine asks with a grin.

I lean across her desk and with my face just inches from her nose I say, "I'm dating the boss's nephew. So you and the rest of the jealous cows better be nice to me or you'll be very, very sorry." Then I give her my sweetest smile and return to my desk.

I am so pleased with myself that I can't stop grinning. I keep looking at the envelope in my handbag. I'm even nice to Billy when he comes to share his news with me. In fact, when he tells me about the evening he has planned with one of his stupid friends, I give him a pound to buy sweets. I've had money from Alan and lunch with Jez. Can this day get any better? I am triumphant. I am back in control.

CHAPTER TWENTY-EIGHT

BILLY

Today is a special day at work because today is review day. Everyone who works for Henderson's has an assessment today so Mr. Henderson can see how hard we're all working. My mum has had my good suit cleaned and I'm wearing a new tie. I've polished my shoes and made sure I've put on clean socks. Yesterday I put the dirty ones back on by mistake. Alan gives everyone their assessment, then hands the reports Mr. Henderson. Then Mr. Henderson calls everybody into his office, one at a time, for a little chat. The only people Alan doesn't assess are Betty and me, because we are special cases. I think that means we work the hardest, but I'm not completely sure.

Betty is called in to see Mr. Henderson first, because she is senior. I think that means she's the oldest and not that she's a senior citizen. When Betty comes out again, she's very happy.

"I've been given a bonus, Billy and a pay rise," she says, "Just in time for my Grandson's graduation. I'll be able to buy him something special now. You've to go in now, Pet. Good luck."

I open the door and walk in. "Hello, Mr. Henderson," I say. "I like your tie."

"Hello Billy," he replies. "Is that a new tie you're wearing?"

I nod my head. I'm pleased he's noticed.

"Well Billy," he continues. "Tell me how you're getting on?

I am not sure what he wants me to say, so I tell him about my new best friend. I tell him how sad David was when his friend left him because he was lonely and how kind he is to me. Then I tell him Jez knows David too, because David is his teacher.

"Jez is always coming over to speak to David," I say. "Jez is a nice boy and he says nice things to David then he smiles at David and winks at him."

"Does Jez visit David's house with you?" Mr. Henderson asks.

"Oh no," I reply, "Never. In fact, when Jez tries to speak to David in the playground, David always sends him back into school. 'Shouldn't you be in a class, Jez?'" he says. "It is a teacher's responsibility to keep his pupils in order."

"Is that what David told you, Billy?" he asks.

"Yes," I reply. "David is a great teacher."

"That's good, Billy," he says. "I'm pleased you have such a sensible, special friend. Does he teach you things as well?"

I think about what he's asked. We're sitting in silence and I feel I must answer something.

"He taught me one thing," I say. "Can you keep a secret?" I ask.

Mr Henderson nods. "Of course I can," he says. "Do you want to tell me about it?"

I really want to tell my secret to somebody because my Mum says if you have a secret that you are worried about, you should tell someone.

"David showed me how to give him a special massage," I say. "But it's a big secret and I told him I wouldn't tell anyone."

"That's okay, Billy," he says. "My lips are sealed." He pretends to zip up his mouth with his hand and it makes me laugh. His face has gone a bit red and I think he should take off his jacket because he looks to warm.

"I'm very pleased with your work, Billy," he says, changing the subject. "I've decided to give you a pay rise. You'll have an extra five pounds a week to spend on yourself and an extra twenty pounds a week to take home to your Mum. However, you must promise me you won't spend all your money on sweets or your Mum will tell me off," he adds.

Before I leave his office, Mr. Henderson wants to discuss David again. He says David and Mum are both wrong about the massage. He says it's okay to do it to yourself as long as it's in a private place where you definitely cannot be seen. He says I mustn't talk about it as it isn't polite. He also says I must never, ever do it to someone else, even if they like it and, if David asks me again, I should just say no.

I am worried that David will be upset if I say no to him but Mr. Henderson says he's sure everything will be okay. He says I did the right thing by telling him because it was a bad secret and you shouldn't have bad secrets.

When I leave his office, I go to see Betty to tell her

about my pay rise. Betty is so pleased for me that she gives me a biscuit and lets me phone my Mum to tell her the good news.

CHAPTER TWENTY-NINE

JEZ

I have to admit I enjoyed myself with Melanie. It's much nicer spending time with middle class scum than with the dregs of the earth. Being a toy boy is a complete change of roll for me, but if she wants to pay to have a younger man fuck her brains out, who am I to argue?

I don't know what sort of scam she's running, but she had a wad of cash to spend the last time she took me out. She certainly didn't get it working for Uncle unless she's fucking him. I can't imagine the old sod fancying Melanie. He's more the Camilla Parker Bowles type. I can just see him jerking off to the sounds of 'Land of Hope and Glory' while drooling over a picture of Camilla. I must find out how Mel's getting her cash because I need another source of income, now the boys are in jail. One way or another, that girl will make money for me. Maybe I'll get her to pose for me so I can take some glamour shots. I'll tell her they're for me to look at when we're apart so I don't get lonely and, if I can get her to do some open leg shots, I can sell them for serious money on the internet.

"Jez, are you joining us today?" My train of thought is interrupted by David, the poofter, Sir.

"It depends what you have in mind, Sir?" I ask, as I stand to face him.

"The Captain's Lady," he replies. "Amongst other things, we are studying The Captain's Lady."

"Doesn't he mind?" I say.

"Doesn't who mind? What are you talking about boy?" he asks. His face is turning red and he's getting flustered. The other boys are beginning to laugh as they anticipate the inevitable. My timing as usual is perfect.

"Why the Captain of course, Sir," I reply.

"Burns, you idiot," he splutters. "The Captain's Lady by Robert Burns."

As the class erupts into chaos, I very deliberately let my hand drift to my crotch and without taking my eyes off David, I smile, lick my lips and simulate having a wank. For a minute I think he's going to hit me. He practically flies across the room at me, but at the last moment he regains control and screams at the class to sit down and shut up.

Just then there is a knock at the door and the Rector's secretary enters the room and gives David a note.

"Jez," he begins. "You are to accompany Miss Higgins to the Rector's office." As I pass by his desk he says, "Do not pass go, do not collect two hundred pounds."

Is that the best you can do? I think. What a wanker.

When I arrive at the Rector's office I knock on the door and I'm invited to enter.

"Ah, Jeremy," he says. "Sit down."

Jeremy. Jeremy. Nobody calls me Jeremy. What an old fart.

"I have received instructions from your guardian," he continues. "He is very concerned for your welfare and about your behaviour. I have had very specific instructions from him that you are to remain in school at lunchtime. You will sit in the dining room where there is supervision. After school you must go straight to your uncle's office. Failure to comply will result in your immediate removal from this school."

I am completely stunned. I sit in silence and try to take in what he's said.

"There is another matter I wish to discuss, Jeremy," he says. "Your uncle has brought to my attention something rather disturbing. It seems you've been targeting Mr. Goldman for some very cruel abuse. Now I know you're well aware of Mr. Goldman's private preferences, but he does not bring his personal life into this school and neither must you. Your treatment of him contravenes his human rights and that will not be tolerated. At seventeen you are old enough and wise enough to understand a person's sexuality is a very personal thing. I will not allow you to bully this fine teacher. Is that clear, Jeremy?"

I nod my head, meekly. I can't speak as my throat is as dry as dust.

"Now make your way to the dining room," he says. "The lunchtime bell is about to ring."

Do not pass go. Do not collect two hundred pounds. I think wryly. Somebody has tipped off my uncle. Somebody has caused me this grief. Who? I wonder. Who could it be?

CHAPTER THIRTY

BILLY

It's the weekend again and I feel great. I've had such a good week because everyone is so pleased with me. Mr. Henderson said if I hadn't been in Marks and Spencer's, Jez might be in jail right now because the police could have thought he was with the bad boys. He also said that because I tell him things, he is able to help Jez to keep out of trouble. Mr. Henderson thinks I'm invaluable and he said, 'Keep up the good work, Billy. You really are the hero of the day, young man.' He called me a hero, me Billy McDaid, a hero. Maybe I really have super powers, but I probably haven't mastered them all yet. You hear about that sort of thing happening all the time. It says so in my comics.

Melanie was pleased with me too and she gave me money for sweets. I think she really will be my girlfriend soon if I keep looking after her. When she's my girlfriend she'll invite me into her house for milk and chocolate biscuits and she might have a pink, fluffy bedroom like Molly. Whenever I think about Melanie, I get that special tickly feeling in my private place. Since Mr. Henderson told me that it's okay to massage it away, I've been massaging quite a lot. Sometimes, when I'm rubbing myself, I think about Melanie wearing the shiny, lacy underwear and I have dirty thoughts about touching her. If she puts her panties on the clothesline again, I think I'll take them home and hide them in my bedroom. Then I'll be able to look at them and touch them whenever I want.

David is very happy since I became his best friend, but he said I shouldn't keep meeting him at the school. He said I should go straight to the bus stop and we can travel together. Now I've got someone to sit beside on the bus home. He also said that, even though we are best friends, I shouldn't put my arm around his shoulders or hold his hand when we are outside because it's not appropriate. I'm still giving him the special massage. I know I shouldn't, but I don't want him to know I told somebody about our special secret. Besides, nobody will ever know and he is my best friend and best friends help each other.

By ten-thirty I've finished doing all the chores for Mum and I decide to go and watch Melanie's house. I have been to watch her quite often, but it's not very comfortable, hiding behind the neighbour's shed and the last time I was there I got quite hungry. Today I've decided to take a fold-up garden chair, a flask of tea, some sandwiches, some comics to read and my pair of binoculars. Then I can pretend I'm on a picnic, just like the one that was on 'The Waltons' on the telly.

"Where are you off to with all those things, Billy?" Mum asks.

"I'm having a picnic in the park," I lie.

"What a nice idea, son," she says. "Would you like some company?"

"No thank you, Mum," I reply. "I'm ready to leave now, bye-bye." I race out of the door, clutching all my stuff, before she gets the chance to follow me.

When I get to the corner of Melanie's street, I meet Frank the postman.

"Off to see Melanie, are you?" he asks.

"Yes," I reply.

"Just one letter today," he says, handing me a square, white envelope.

"It feels like a card. Is it her birthday?"

I don't know if it's her birthday, but I feel I should know, so I change the subject.

"I'm going for a picnic," I say. "I'm going for a picnic and to visit Melanie."

"How nice for you Billy and if that sun gets any hotter, you might see more of her than you bargained for," he says, then laughs.

I don't really know what's funny but I laugh anyway.

"I must go now or I'll be late," I say. I don't want Frank to see me go into the neighbour's garden.

"Goodbye Billy, have fun," he replies and I hurry along the street ahead of him.

I manage to slip into the garden without being seen as nobody is about. There's plenty of room for my chair behind the shed and I arrange my flask and sandwiches on the ground beside me. I wear my binoculars round my neck and hold my comics so they don't get dirty. I spend quite a long time looking through my binoculars and I'm surprised how much I can see. I can see right inside some of the houses and I can see people moving around. If only I had one of those special microphones that James Bond has, I could hear what they were saying.

I've almost finished reading my comics and I've drunk all my tea and eaten most of my sandwiches when the back door of the house opens and a lady comes out carrying plates and cutlery. She places everything on a table on the patio then goes back inside. Over the next few minutes she brings out more things for the table and a man comes out and puts coals on the bar-be-cue and lights it.

They can't see me because I'm hidden behind the shed. Maybe I have become invisible. Maybe my Superhero powers are getting stronger and that's why they don't know I'm here. I decide to test them. Every so often I jump out from behind the shed, wave my hands then jump back again. I jump out and back three times and still they don't see me. Then I sit down again and watch them through my binoculars some more.

After a while, another couple of people arrive and I think they must be lunch guests. I'm reading my comic when suddenly a huge Alsatian dog runs up to me. It's barking and barking and jumping from side to side.

"Noooo," I shout, "Noooo."

I don't want it to bite me. I'm holding my chair in front of me to keep the dog back. Everyone runs up to me, they are all shouting and I'm frightened. One of the men calls the dog to him and grabs its collar.

"Who are you? What are you doing here?" the lady of the house asks. I don't know what to say. I'm no longer invisible.

"What are you doing here?" she demands.

"I'm having a picnic," I answer, and stare at the ground.

"This is private property," the man of the house says. "You can't have a picnic here."

"He's simple, John," the lady says. "Go easy on him."

"You'll need to leave now," he says. "I'll help you gather up your things and I'll show you to the front gate."

I don't say anything, I just nod and gather my stuff. Then I follow the man past the big dog to the front of the garden and out of the gate. As I stand on the pavement, I hear the people talking and laughing. I'm so glad that Melanie didn't see me. If the big dog hadn't arrived, I would have stayed invisible. Dogs see things that people can't see, like ghosts and evil spirits and invisible Superheroes.

I still have Melanie's letter that Frank gave me to deliver. If I hurry home Mum will still be in town with Aunty Mabel and I'll be able to open it and read it without being disturbed. When I arrive home, I lift the letter opener and go upstairs to my room. I carefully open the envelope and discover it holds a card as Frank thought, but it's not a Birthday card and it has a cheque inside. There's a picture of a teddy bear on the front and no verse inside. It reads……

Dear Melanie,

Please find enclosed my cheque for £600 so you can take care of the baby.

I'm sorry things didn't work out between us, but I'm pleased you're being sensible about the situation.

Neither of us wants to be tied down at this stage of our lives.

I hope everything goes well for you.

Please let me know when everything is over and we can meet for lunch if you like.

Good Luck

Stephen

I read it over and over again. Melanie must be collecting money to help a poor baby. I think she's very kind and Stephen is very generous, whoever Stephen might be. I know this is a letter Melanie has to receive or she won't be able to use Stephen's cheque for the baby. I must make sure I put it through her letterbox right away.

I've often heard of people making anonymous donations to charity and I decide I'll make a donation because it's a good cause. I take two pound coins out of my money box and put them in the envelope with the card and the cheque from Stephen. Then I re-seal the envelope with sticky tape and print on the outside, 'I know what you are doing'. Melanie will get such a surprise when she gets my anonymous donation. I'm sure she'll be very pleased and she'll wonder who sent her the money.

CHAPTER THIRTY-ONE

BELLA

Mabel has done nothing but moan all week. It's not as if I've asked her to do any extra work, I've simply asked her to clean thoroughly. My nephew, Professor Alexander Herbert-Smyth is coming to stay for the weekend and he suffers from dust mite allergy. He must not come across a single dust mite in this house or I will never live it down.

The professor is attending a convention at the Marriot Hotel in Glasgow and he has graciously chosen to stay with me, even though he could opt for a four-star hotel. As he's an Oxford professor and the guest speaker at the convention, the sky's the limit as far as his expenses go. Mabel spitefully says he's probably keeping the expenses while staying here for free, but I have assured her that he's honest and honourable and he's staying here because he loves me and wants to spend time with me. She's just jealous because she doesn't have a loving nephew. She has nobody apart from her stupid friend with the idiot son, whereas my relative is an Oxford professor with an impeccable pedigree. It's true, his name is really Alexander Herbert Smith, but being an Oxford man,

Herbert-Smyth has so much more character. Nobody needs to know Herbert is really his middle name and not part of his surname and it is Smith with an 'I' not Smyth with a 'y'. Nobody in Mabel's social group would give two figs, but with our social standing, a double-barrelled name is more appropriate for his position.

Every inch of his room has been cleaned even the walls have been wiped down with a damp cloth and I've bought new, 'hypoallergenic' bedding for his bed. Mabel thinks I'm stupid to spend all that money on bedding for one weekend but it was only £120 and I can afford it. It's two weeks wages for Mabel. I pointed it out to her, that if I didn't have to pay her £60 a week on top of giving her room and board, I'd be a wealthy woman and the whole house could be 'hypoallergenic'. As usual she said nothing but stormed off in a sulk. What could she say? She knows I'm right.

I could never allow myself to be in her position, living off someone else's charity. I have never understood why she hasn't found some wealthy man to marry her. She's still an attractive woman in a common sort of way and she's an adequate housekeeper. I'm sure some man would marry her.

At last I hear Mabel's key in the door. I hope she's managed to get everything on the list I gave her. There are some things you can only get at Marks and Spencer's and Alexander will probably want a snack when he arrives after his long journey.

"Put the kettle on, Mabel dear," I call, when I hear her enter the hall. "I'm ready for afternoon tea."

"Let me get my coat off first, please," she replies. "Town was chock-a-block and I'm exhausted. Besides, this is supposed to be my day off and I've already spent half of it shopping for you. I think it's you who should be making me a cup of tea."

"Oh really, Mabel, what a fuss," I reply. "Sometimes I think it is I who works for you."

She storms off into the kitchen and I hear the sound of the kettle being filled.

Mabel has just brought in the tea when there's a ring of the doorbell. Alexander has arrived. When I open the door he bows deeply, takes my hand in his, and kisses it. Then he produces his other hand from behind his back clutching a single red rose.

"For you, dear Aunty Belle," he says.

"Oh, Alexander," I reply. "How charming, what a lovely gesture. Don't you think so, Mabel?"

"Yes, lovely," she replies flatly. "There's another rose exactly like it in the kitchen," she whispers to me. "They were selling them at the station for a pound each, to raise money for the Children's Hospice. He's a bit cheap if that's all he's brought you."

I am bristling with anger. Mabel's jealousy is becoming too much for me to bear.

"We will have tea, thank you, Mabel," I say, "Set the tray down on the small table by the window. You may take tea in your room or in the kitchen. Alexander and I have some things to talk over in private."

She storms off in another sulk and I hear her banging about in the kitchen, but I don't care. Alexander is my guest, not hers.

After his tea, Alexander excuses himself and goes to his room for a rest before getting ready for the convention. At 5.30 I have Mabel run a bath for him and wake him up with a cup of tea. He comes downstairs at seven looking very grand in his dinner suit and bow tie. His taxi is booked for 7.15 so he has just enough time to sip a small sherry and have me to run a clothes brush over his collar before he is gone, leaving the exotic scent of his expensive cologne in his wake.

I have given Alexander the spare key as Mabel has flatly refused to wait up for him. I must have my nine hours sleep or I'll wake up with a headache, but Mabel often stays up very late. She's simply being awkward. If it was her nephew I'm sure she'd wait up and make him some supper, without complaint. She knows I'm unhappy with her and we sit in virtual silence all evening before retiring early to our rooms.

I don't feel as if I've had much sleep when all hell breaks loose. There is a loud bang, bang, bang at the front door. I jump up, grab my dressing gown and reach the door alongside Mabel.

"Who's there?" Mabel calls.

We hear laughter then another bang, bang on the door.

"It's me, Aunty, let me in," a drunken voice calls.

"We'd better open the door before he wakes the whole street," Mabel says. "He's drunk," she adds smugly. When she opens the door, we are greeted by a very drunken Alexander and a rather scantily clad woman. He's leaning against the wall of the house with his shirt open to the waist and she's clutching some ten-pound notes in her hand, while trying to do up his trousers. There's a taxi with its engine running waiting at the gate.

"You were great, Jackie," he slurs, "Worth every penny of the fifty pounds."

There's an embarrassing silence as we absorb the implication of what he's just said. Then Jackie gives him a peck on the cheek, turns and runs to the waiting taxi, leaving Mabel and I to cope with Alexander.

"What have you done? Oh Alexander, how could you?" I say, my cheeks burning with embarrassment. "I suppose you're enjoying this?" I say to Mabel as we struggle to get him through the front door.

"I haven't done anything, Aunty," he says. "Jackie did everything. She's a very naughty girl. She is a professional, a pro, a prostitute," he adds, laughing.

"You won't find this so funny tomorrow," Mabel reproaches him. "When you have a hangover and you have to apologise to your Aunty."

"Aunty, shmanty, doesn't wear panties," he replies and laughs. Then he turns to me, "Give us a kiss," he says, as he burps alcoholic fumes in my face.

Somehow the three of us stumble upstairs towards his room. We have managed to make it to the bathroom on the landing when he suddenly says, "sick". Mabel propels him through the door and closes it behind him. Almost immediately we hear the sound of retching.

"That's the best thing for him," she says. "It will get the alcohol out of his system. I'm going to my bed now," she adds.

I watch her close her bedroom door then I high tail it to my room in case Alexander comes out of the bathroom and I have to tend to him myself. I have a very fitful night tossing and turning this way and that until I finally fall asleep in the early hours of the morning. I awaken at ten and I'm still tired. When I enter the kitchen, I see Mabel washing out the mop in a bucket and, to my relief, there's no sign of Alexander.

"He's gone," she says. "I've being cleaning vomit

off the bathroom for the last hour and a half. He managed to be sick everywhere, the toilet, the sink, the bath, even the walls were covered and he made no attempt to clean up. He might be posh but he has no class," she adds with a smirk. "That note is for you," she says, pointing to a folded piece of paper on the table.

I lift Alexander's letter and read...

Unfortunate about last night, somebody must have spiked my drink. I had to leave early so I didn't want to disturb you.

Kindest Regards

Alexander

"No apology I take it," Mabel says. "His sort never apologise. They are too arrogant."

"He said someone spiked his drink," I say, lamely.

"It must have been the same person who hired the prostitute for him," she throws back at me.

I feel my face redden with shame.

"What do you want done with your 'hypoallergenic' bedding," she asks, nodding at the two black bin bags standing in the corner of the kitchen. "He peed the bed. It's jolly lucky that I put on the mattress protector."

I'm absolutely disgusted. "Put the bags at the bin," I reply. "And I don't want to hear any more on the matter, Mabel."

I leave the kitchen and head back to my room as I can't face breakfast yet. I'm so angry with Alexander. He was to be my heir, I think ruefully. I certainly won't be leaving him this house or my money now, not after his disgusting behaviour, but that leaves me with a predicament as neither do I wish to bequeath it to Mabel, whatever I told her. In the end, I decide to telephone Mr. Henderson, my solicitor and make an appointment to change my will. I will not leave everything I've worked hard for all my life to unworthy or ungrateful people. Mabel will never know I'm leaving her nothing unless I die first and, if that happens, I'll be past caring and Alexander must not be allowed to fritter away my life savings on an excessive lifestyle. I have other ideas for my money which will please me much better.

CHAPTER THIRTY-TWO

BILLY

I am so happy that it's Monday. It's a new week and I can forget all about my bad time with the big dog and Melanie's neighbours. I managed to put Melanie's letter through her letterbox without being seen so that's another dangerous mission over.

"You're going to Brannigan's today, Pet," Betty says. "If I plan your route properly, you'll be able to pop home for lunch."

"I'll be able to see Clare and Susan," I reply. "I really like them, they're very nice girls. If I take my sandwiches with me, I can eat them in the park and feed the crusts to the ducks."

"That's nice, Pet," Betty says. "But wouldn't you rather have lunch with your Mum? You can phone her if you like."

"She's going out for lunch with my Aunty Mabel," I lie. I spend enough time with my Mum I think, far too much time.

Clare and Susan are both at Brannigan's when I arrive. They're always nice to me and they always talk to me.

"Hello there, Billy." Clare says. "We haven't seen

you for a while. Are you still seeing Melanie Coulson?" she asks. Susan looks at her and they both laugh. They are always laughing. They're such friendly, happy girls.

"Of course I'm still seeing Melanie," I reply. "I see her every day."

"Oh, how nice for you Billy," Clare says. "What do you two get up to then?"

"I help Melanie," I reply. I help her and I look after her."

"In what way do you help her Billy?" Susan questions. "Do you carry her shopping and take her hand crossing the street?"

I don't know what to tell them. I stare at the ground and try to think of something to say that will impress them.

"Cat got your tongue?" Clare asks.

"I helped her with money for a poor baby," I reply pleased I've thought of something.

They exchange glances. "What poor baby is this?" Susan asks

"Perhaps we can help too," Clare says.

"You can't help," I say. "It's too late. All the donations are in."

"How much did she get?" Susan asks.

"A man called Stephen gave her £600 to take care of the baby and I gave her two pounds from my moneybox. But you mustn't tell her it was me who gave her the two pounds because I was anonymous."

"That was very generous of you," Clare says. "Wasn't that very generous, Susan?"

Susan agrees, then they quickly sign for the letters I've brought and shoo me out of the door.

"We have to have a private talk, Billy, just Clare

and me. You understand, don't you Billy?" Susan says, as she starts to close the door.

"Of course I understand," I reply. "Brannigan's business is private."

Before I leave, I look through the glass of the door and I see Susan sitting on Clare's desk. They are talking excitedly about something. Their hands are moving as they speak and they are laughing. My Mum says girls love to gossip and she's right, if Clare and Susan are anything to go by.

My next call is at Watson and Bell at Muirend and when I arrive there, Marjory is making a cup of tea.

"Are you in a hurry, Billy?" she asks. "Have you time for a wee cup of tea? The boss is in court today so if you've got the time, I'd like the company. It's been dead quiet here."

"I'd like a cup, thank you," I reply, "Two sugars and a chocolate biscuit please."

Marjory laughs, "Sit down over there and I'll bring our tea over," she says, pointing to a big, comfy looking armchair. "What's new with you, Billy?" she asks.

I tell her all about Melanie and how she is going to be my girlfriend and how I helped her with the poor baby. She tells me all about her new boyfriend called Stephen.

"That's funny," I say. "That's the same name as the man who gave Melanie £600 to take care of the baby."

Marjory's hand starts to shake and her cup rattles in the saucer.

"My Stephen used to go out with Melanie Coulson," she says. "He said he only took her out to dinner twice. Surely the money couldn't have come from him. Surely it couldn't have been his baby."

"No, Marjory," I say. "It was a charity baby, like you see on the telly. I gave Melanie two pounds from my moneybox."

"Did you see Melanie's Stephen? Do you know what he looks like?

"No," I reply. "I only saw his card. It had teddies on the front." There is a long silence and I think maybe I shouldn't have said anything about the poor baby. As soon as I finish my tea, Marjory whisks away my cup.

"I have to make a phone call so you'd better be on your way," she says.

I wave goodbye as I go out of the door, but she is already on the phone and she doesn't wave back.

When I get back to the office, I see Mrs. Worthington waiting to go into Mr. Henderson's room. Why is she here, I wonder? Is she going to say bad things about me? I'm sure she said bad things about me to my Mum. I haven't done anything bad. I'm sure I haven't, except maybe the special massage for David, but she couldn't know about that. I'm sure she couldn't know.

It's nearly time for me to go home. When I get to the bus stop I can ask David about Mrs. Worthington. I worry about her because Aunty Mabel told me she needs to be watched. He'll know if I have anything to worry about because he's clever. He's a teacher and teachers know everything.

CHAPTER THIRTY-THREE

DAVID

Another Monday over at last, how I hate Mondays. I feel as if I'm under scrutiny all the time. Wherever I turn the Rector is watching me, and Jez never seems to leave the school. It is my month to supervise the dining hall and Jez is always there, watching me, glowering at me or blowing me kisses and, when I leave the school, Billy is always around. I'm like some pet that's being loved to death. It's claustrophobic, stifling. I'm suffocating, drowning in all the attention. My life was so easy before, but I didn't realise it.

When Mark and I were together I had love in my life and a job that was tolerable. I had free time and privacy and I wasn't lonely. Now I know how a lab rat must feel, trapped, observed, isolated, miserable and frightened. I'm all of these things, but above all I'm frightened, very, very frightened. What have I done to deserve this misery?

I want to be rid of Jez before I do something I'll regret. I have to be rid of that beautiful, cruel, little bastard because I want him so much I ache. I dream about him. When I'm with Billy I pretend it is Jez's hand touching me. I'm like some pathetic teenage girl with a crush on a pop star.

As for Billy, I must push him away from me before someone finds out what I've done. How could I have been so stupid? I'm a teacher for Christ's sake, I have responsibilities. What on earth was I thinking about getting involved with a retarded man? Now I can't get rid of him. I don't want his big, meaty, fumbling hands on me anymore, but how can I get rid of him? He might tell someone, then what would I do? Maybe I should quit my job and go overseas again, God, what a mess, what a bloody mess.

I'm standing at the bus stop, deep in thought, when I'm aware that somebody has moved beside me and is standing so close our arms are touching.

"Hello, Sir," a voice says. "How's it hanging?"

It's Jez. My heart skips a beat.

"I get the impression you'd like to see more of me," he continues. "The Rector made it very clear you'd like to have me around you all the time. So here I am. Is this close enough for you, Sir?"

He squeezes closer to me so that his leg is touching mine. I begin to tremble and my dick is like a ramrod. Beads of perspiration form on my brow.

"What's this all about, Jez?" I manage to say, as I sidestep away from him. "What are you talking about?"

He looks slightly puzzled. "I'm talking about you getting the Rector to force me to stay in school at lunchtime," he says. "It must have been you because you're the only poofter teacher I've been winding up."

"I don't know what you're talking about," I reply.

"I've said nothing to him. Why would someone like me draw attention to himself? Think about it, Jez. You're not stupid."

Just then Billy gallops up to the stop. "Hello Jez, hello David," he says, grinning like a Cheshire cat. "I'm so glad to see you both together. Now I can talk to you both at the same time. Melanie will be coming to the bus stop soon and we can all travel together. I can sit beside David because he's my best friend and Jez and Melanie can sit on the seat in front. Then I'll be able to see everyone," he says, excitedly.

Jez and I exchange glances. "This isn't over yet," he says to me. "We'll talk again." He turns to Billy. "I'm off to my uncle's office, big man, bye, Billy." He turns to me and salutes. "Bye, Sir. Keep your pecker up," and he laughs as he walks away. Billy's face looks worried as he says to me, "What's a pecker? Is it your private thing? Does he know about the special massage? Did you tell him?"

"Shush, Billy," I say. "Keep your voice down," I hiss and my eyes dart about to see if anyone could have overheard him. "It's just a saying, Billy. It doesn't mean anything. You know you mustn't talk about us to anybody. Not a soul."

"Not a soul," he repeats, but his eyes look guilty and I feel very vulnerable.

What a mess, I think. What a bloody mess.

Billy prattles on and on and I'm relieved to get off the bus. I manage to persuade him not to get off with me by lying about a dental appointment. When I get back to my flat and stare at the empty rooms with their dull, depressing walls, I can't stand it anymore. Racking sobs overwhelm me as I sit on the edge of my bed and contemplate my future. I am bereft. Mr.

Henderson has said something to the Rector about me concerning Jez. But what has he heard and where and who did he hear it from? Nothing has happened between us except Jez's tortuous cruelty and his contemptuous remarks. Jez, it seems, is as mystified as I am.

Where do I go from here? Is there any future for me? I know I've no chance of promotion and it's clear I'm merely tolerated by the Rector under sufferance. I'm the token gay just as Mr. Singh is the token foreigner and Mrs. Bell is the token female.

I'm so lost and lonely I actually let my mind speculate about the easiest way to kill myself. Just when I have narrowed it down to an overdose of ' Paracetamol' or throwing myself under the 9.20 from Queens Park to Glasgow Central, the telephone rings. Maybe there's hope for me yet, I think. Please, please let it be a friendly voice I pray, even if it's a wrong number. I need to hear a friendly voice.

CHAPTER THIRTY-FOUR

BILLY

My Mum says it's been an Indian summer but it's definitely over now. I haven't actually seen any Indians yet. You don't expect to see Indians in Glasgow these days and I wonder if they really have red skins and wear feathers in their hair. I did see a man in a cowboy hat one day. Some boys were running behind him, shouting, 'Show us your horse Mister,' and 'My sister's going out with an Indian would you come and shoot the bastard?' so there must be Indians somewhere. Maybe they go to East Kilbride for the winter. My mum says you can get everything in East Kilbride. Maybe they put up their wigwams in Calderglen Country Park. That would be a good place for their horses because the park keeper could help to look after them.

I'm standing outside Debenhams in Argyle Street, thinking all these thoughts while, watching the window display, people change the window from a boring clothes display to a great Halloween scene. Suddenly a hand grabs my shoulder and I jump.

"Found you at last, fuckwit," a voice says. "You canny hide from big Tam forever."

It's one of the bad boys and I'm scared. I try to pull away but he grips my arm,

"Don't even think about bolting, fuckwit," he says. "You and me are going to have a wee chat."

He forces me to walk round the corner, off the main road and into a lane behind Debenhams.

"I want some information from you and I want it now," he says. "First of all, empty your pockets, I need money."

"I haven't got any money," I reply. "I've only got my bus pass." I'm not going to tell him about my emergency money because this is an emergency and I might need it.

"Fuck it," he says. "I can't believe my friends got lifted because of a moron like you. I suppose that wee shite Jez got lifted too, but his rich uncle probably got him off.

"Jez is not a bad boy," I say, jumping to his defence. "He's in school. He's not in jail."

"Oh, is that right? He must be avoiding me then. He must think, because my friends are in the jail, he can forget about the money he owes us."

I'm sorry I spoke. I don't want the bad boy to find Jez.

Suddenly he slaps my face hard and I begin to cry.

"Listen to me, fuckwit," he says. "I want your full attention. Have I got your full attention?"

I nod my head, my cheek is burning and I can't stop crying.

"Where will I find Jez?" he asks. "You work for his uncle and you seem to know about him. Tell me where I'll find him."

"He's in school every week day and after school

he goes to the office to meet his uncle. I don't know what he does at the weekend or in the evening," I reply.

"You're not much fucking use then are you, fuckwit?" he says.

I stand frozen to the spot with fear. Tam grabs the lapels of my jacket and drags me to the ground. I curl into a ball and try to protect my head as he stomps on me and kicks me.

"I'll be back for you when my friends get out of jail," he threatens. "I'll be back for you and I'll find that wee shite, Jez."

The kicking finally stops and I peer out from behind my hands. He is gone. I manage to stand up. Nothing seems to be broken but my face feels puffy and sore and my body feels bruised. My clothes are dirty and wet but I still have my briefcase and my bus pass and my emergency money. I walk slowly to the end of the lane and look about. When I am sure that he's definitely gone, I run back to the safety of the main road. People walking by are staring at me and a woman comes over to talk to me.

"Are you all right?" she asks. "Have you been mugged? You look a bit dazed."

I'm so relieved someone is looking after me I begin to cry again. The lady takes my arm and walks me over to the wall of the shop then she takes her mobile phone out of her pocket and phones the police.

When the police arrive, they ask me my name and address and get me to tell them what has happened. Then they take me in the police car back to the office. Everyone is fussing around me at the office and someone phones my mum. After I have a cup of strong, sweet tea Mr. Henderson comes to talk to me.

"How are you feeling, Billy?" he asks.

"Much better, thanks," I reply.

"That's good Billy, get your coat and I'll drive you home to your Mum. She's expecting you," he adds.

I feel really excited because I'm going to travel in Mr. Henderson's Mercedes.

"You're a good lad, Billy," he says, as he helps me into the car. "I wish things could have been different. I knew your Mum when we were younger, you know? I knew her very well. We dated for a while before she married your father. I wish things could have been different for us all."

I'm not sure whether I'm meant to answer him because I'm not sure what he's talking about, so I settle down in the big leather seat and stare out of the window. If I look carefully, I might see some Indians on the way home.

CHAPTER THIRTY-FIVE

MELANIE

What a carry on, what a fuss. It's bad enough that I didn't start my lunch until 1.30 without all this rubbish when I get back. I've had Mrs. McDaid bawling on the phone for the last twenty minutes. I told her Billy was okay and he certainly didn't need to go to the hospital for a check-up but the old bag still insisted on talking to Mr. Henderson. I wish someone else had been given the job of phoning her. She kept asking me if his head was injured, as if that would make any difference. He's already retarded. Maybe she thinks a head injury would improve him. Maybe she thinks it would dislodge something in his brain and he'd be normal.

I've got a note on my desk to return a call to Marjorie Atkins at Watson and Bell because she called when I was at lunch. I wonder what she wants. I'm sure the papers I sent her this morning were in order. Billy must have delivered them because he'd already returned to the city centre when he was mugged. I dial the number and the phone is answered almost immediately.

"Watson and Bell, Miss Atkins speaking, how

may I help you?" Marjorie answers.

"Marjory, hello, it's Melanie Coulson from Henderson's, you called me earlier. Is there a problem with the papers for the Taylor case?"

"This has nothing to do with work," she says. "I hear you're pregnant and you're going to have an abortion. Is that true?"

"W what," I stammer. "Who told you that?" My mind is racing and my heart is thumping. How did she hear this?

"Never mind who told me," she continues. "I just want to know the truth. Is it my Stephen's baby? Did he give you money to get rid of it?"

"I haven't the foggiest idea what you're talking about," I lie. "Someone has obviously been rattling your chains. You must excuse me now as this has nothing to do with work and I'm not allowed personal calls. You should get your facts right before you go making these sorts of accusations. If I hear any more about it, I'll be raising an action for slander." I bang down the receiver before she gets the chance to say any more.

I wonder if she phoned to confront me before calling Stephen. I quickly dial his number because I must warn him in case he puts his foot in it. He answers it on the eighth ring just as I'm about to give up.

"Stephen, it's Melanie, I'm sorry to phone you at work. Has Marjory called you yet?"

"Why would Marjory phone me at work?" he asks. "Is something wrong?"

"Have you told her about us?" I demand. "Have you told her anything about the baby?"

"She knows nothing about the baby," he replies. "Of course I've said nothing, what's going on?"

"She's just off the phone, demanding to know if it's yours," I reply, "Someone has said something to her."

"Jesus Aitch Christ," he says. "What did you tell her?"

"I denied everything, of course and you must do the same. I will get to the bottom of this. Someone is talking about me and I'm going to find out who it is. Are you absolutely positive you haven't told anyone?"

"Of course I'm positive," he says. It's not something I'd boast about. If we both keep denying everything, it will be a nine-day wonder."

I sincerely hope he's right because I'm expecting a cheque from Ben any day and I don't want anything to jeopardise it. I'm about to hang up when Stephen asks.

"Could anyone have read the card I sent you with the cheque? Did you leave it lying around anywhere?"

"No of course not," I reply. "Nobody touches my mail."

After he's off the phone I have a heavy feeling in my chest caused by a nagging fear. Somebody had touched my mail. The words, 'I know what you are doing' were printed on the outside of the envelope, but I was so happy to get the cheque I ignored it and threw the envelope in the bin. Then there were the two pound coins I found inside the envelope. What was that all about? I feel scared. Who could it be? Someone is watching me and tampering with my mail.

"Are you planning to do any work, Melanie, or are you just going to sit and daydream?"

Alan's voice breaks my chain of thought.

"S sorry," I stammer, and I quickly open the file on my desk.

Alan, I think to myself. Maybe it's Alan who's said something. No, it can't be, I dismiss. He wouldn't want anyone to know he's been involved with me and he couldn't touch my mail.

I can't wait for five o'clock so I can leave the office. When I get into reception, Jez is there.

"Your uncle's not here," I tell him. "Billy got mugged so your uncle is driving him home."

"Shame about Billy, but I'm glad the old bastard isn't here. It's the best news I've had all day," he says. "Come on Melly, I'll walk you to the bus, I've got a business idea to discuss with you."

"Wait for me, Jez," I reply. "I've just got to nip to the ladies before I leave."

When I enter, Geraldine is standing at the sink applying her lipstick. She eyes me in the mirror.

"I was speaking to Clare from Brannigan's earlier," she says. "It seems the whole of Clarkston is talking about you."

"What are you talking about Geraldine?" I reply. "Are you spreading more of your poison?"

"Putting on a bit of weight, Melanie? Too many buns in the proverbial oven perhaps?"

Before I get a chance to reply, she's out of the door. What a bitch, I think. I can't believe what she's said. First Marjory from Watson and Bell and now Clare from Brannigan's, how many more people are talking about me, I wonder? Who has told them? How could they possibly know? The words that were printed on the envelope come back to haunt me, 'I know what you are doing.' But who knows and what do they want from me? I'm scared, what will I do?

CHAPTER THIRTY-SIX

BILLY

Mr. Henderson parks the Mercedes right outside my house, right outside my gate so the neighbours can see me arriving. Mum is looking out for us and, as we climb out of the car, she opens the front door.

"Thank you for bringing him home, Peter," she says. "I was so worried about him. Imagine someone mugging a poor soul like Billy. Couldn't they see how he is?"

"He's a fine, strapping, young man, Mary. Maybe it wasn't immediately apparent to the mugger," Mr. Henderson replies. "Besides so many of them are spaced out on drugs these days they don't know what they're doing. Billy said something about Indians to the police, so perhaps it was some sort of racial attack."

"There are no Indians in the office and I didn't see any on the way home. They must have gone to East Kilbride," I say, trying to take part in the conversation.

"That's right, Dear," Mum says. "They've all gone

away. You're safe now. Go into the sitting room and I'll be in soon with a nice cup of tea."

She turns to Mr. Henderson and says. "Poor soul it's been quite an ordeal for him."

"How are you managing, Mary?" Mr. Henderson asks. "Are you all right for money?"

"I'm alright Peter," she replies. "Billy's pay rise will help of course. It's not cheap taking care of him. He's a big lad and he's heavy on clothes and shoes."

"Do you get the chance to socialise much? Have you friends to help you?" he asks.

"Socialise," she replies. "Not really. I see my friend Mabel quite often and I'm in the local Resident's Association. The highlight of my week is going into town on a Saturday afternoon with Mabel. Billy makes people feel uneasy so it's been difficult to keep friends. He was so big when he was a child, he sometimes inadvertently hurt other children and when he got excited, he was very loud. He still is," she says laughing.

"I'm sorry about the way things worked out. You know I've always done my best to help you," Mr. Henderson says.

"I know Peter, you're a good man. You've always done your best by us," Mum replies.

I'm fed up listening to their boring conversation so I put the telly on to drown them out. There's an advert on the telly for something called 'Plan International'. A lady is saying if you send them fourteen pounds a month you can foster a child like 'Patricia'. That's probably what Melanie needed the money for. She's probably paying the whole lot at once instead of paying it up. It's really great you can pay it up and fourteen pounds a month isn't too much. When Mum bought the new sofa she had to pay it up at fifty pounds a month and it only had to come from Clydebank. Melanie's baby will have to travel from another country.

I wonder if they'll send her foster baby soon. On 'Pet Rescue' when someone fosters an animal, the RSPCA man delivers it in a special box in his van. I don't suppose they'll put a baby in a box in a van. Perhaps they'll have a special delivery person who'll bring it in a pram. Maybe Frank the postman will bring it. He sometimes makes special deliveries. He carries lots of important things. I must ask him, I think to myself. Maybe one day I could work for 'Plan International' and deliver babies. I've already got experience delivering very important letters and secret papers.

Mum brings in the tea. "'Rugrats' is on the other channel Billy, if you'd like to turn round. You usually like that programme," she says. I love the programme because it's all about babies. I think babies are very funny. When Melanie's foster baby arrives, she might bring it in to the office and I'll get to play with it at lunchtime. I can't wait. I just can't wait.

CHAPTER THIRTY-SEVEN

JEZ

I'm very relieved Uncle Peter isn't here to meet me but a bit concerned about what Melanie told me about Billy. It's clear to me he's had a run in with Big Tam and I know Tam will be looking for me because I owe him and his friends money. I don't really want to pay them because they let me down on the last job. It wasn't my fault they got lifted so I don't see why I should pay for goods I didn't receive. There was nothing I could've done to help them, not after Billy's shouting drew attention to them. If they'd just dumped the damn stuff instead of running, they would have been okay, but they've never had much in the way brains. Anyway, they'll probably think I got lifted too as I scarpered before they were brought back into the store. When I see them, I can tell them Uncle Peter got me off. They'll believe me because he's actually quite well known and a respected lawyer amongst the criminal fraternity. I'll just keep stalling them about the money because what can they do? I'm their best source of income, without me they're fucked. I return my attention to Melanie.

"I've been thinking about that scam you're running," I say.

"You haven't told anyone, have you Jez?" she asks.

"No, of course not," I reply. "You seem upset. What's wrong?"

Melanie tells me all about her day and I understand why she's so jumpy

"I'd like to tell you about my money making idea," I say. "We can't talk out here in the street. How about a coffee and something to eat? I'm starving."

"Thanks Jez," she replies. "I don't really feel like going home just now. What do you fancy to eat?"

"Something quick and filling, like a burger and fries, but I don't want to go to McDonalds or Burger King because they're too crowded and too public. I don't want us to be overheard," I reply.

"An intimate burger bar, that would be a novelty," she says laughing. "Actually, if you don't mind a bit of a walk, I know the very place, it's called 'Wishbones' and it's in High Street. It's like an American diner, but more intimate, and the food is pretty good."

As we make our way to the restaurant Melanie uses my mobile to phone her Mum and let her know she'll be late home. Melanie isn't wrong about 'Wishbones' and we are soon seated at a discreetly positioned table at the back of the restaurant and I'm tucking into the best burger and fries I've ever tasted. The waitress is a bit of all right too. Melanie orders a chicken salad.

"I have to watch my figure," she says with a smile. "I don't want to end up looking pregnant."

"While we're on the subject, that's what I want to talk to you about," I begin. "At the moment you're making £600 a pop from the punters. How would you like to make three times that?" I have her full attention so I continue. "I could arrange for you to have a date with a more affluent client. The person I have in mind is a professional footballer who's a friend of my Dads."

"A famous footballer?" she asks.

"I'll say," I reply. "He plays for a Premier League team. Are you interested?"

"Tell me more," she says, excitedly.

"I know he often plays away from home, so to speak," I continue. "He talks to my Dad about it and he's always showing off to me. I know he's going to the Sports Award Dinner at the Hilton Hotel on Saturday and I just happen to have two tickets for it. My parents are out of town so it would be a shame for their tickets to go to waste. I plan to set it up so we sit beside him. I know one of the organisers managers and it shouldn't be too difficult. I'll book a room under a false name so you have somewhere to take him. What do you say? Are we on for it?"

"How do you know he'll go for it? He might not fancy me."

"He'll fancy you, don't you worry about that," I reply. "You'll look like a million dollars. We'll get your hair styled by Justin and you'll be wearing a slinky designer number. You'll be able to touch his thigh and his dick under the table because you'll be sitting right beside him. Of course he'll fancy you. I'll keep him well oiled with scotch just to make sure he's in the mood. When you invite him to your room, he'll be gagging for it."

"But I don't know him. How will I get the money out of him," she asks.

"You leave that side of things to me," I reply. "I'll

get the money out of him no bother. That's why we're going to be partners."

"I don't own any designer clothes, Jez," she says. "I'm not in that league. What will I wear?"

"Don't worry Cinderella, you will go to the ball," I reassure her. "We'll use my Mum's account to take clothes out on approval. I think a little 'Versace' number should do the trick. After the dinner we'll simply hand them back and say they weren't suitable. My Mum has done it loads of times. She buys so much stuff from them, they put up with her. On the whole she buys much more than she returns."

"So let me get this straight," she says. "I'll be there as your partner but I'll spend the night in our room with him. What about his wife, where will she be?"

"She'll be at home because she's pregnant. She's a good Catholic girl and she's always pregnant, poor cow. This will be baby number four. He'll do anything to preserve the image of a good man who's committed to his family. That's what his manager and his fans want to believe. In reality he's a cokehead and a drunk and he probably won't even manage to get it up, but the good news is he'll never remember in the morning so we'll be okay."

"Will I be safe, Jez?" she asks. "What if he gets violent? I don't know anything about him or what he's capable of."

"Don't worry Melanie you'll be fine. Besides I'll have the second key and I'll be right outside the door," I assure her. "I'll bung the night porter so he'll keep out of the way. Everything will be fine. We'll go shopping for your dress tomorrow. Phone your work and say you're sick and I'll phone in sick too. I definitely think you'll look hot in 'Versace'. What do you think?"

"I think you're mad," she replies, laughing. "Utterly mad, but I love it. I just love it."

CHAPTER THIRTY-EIGHT

BILLY

I hope Melanie is okay because she wasn't in the office yesterday. Geraldine was talking to the other girls and she said maybe it was baby day. Alan got really angry and he told her to shut up and he said he wouldn't tolerate idle, malicious gossip. He said if he hears any more about it she can look for another job. I don't like Geraldine because she laughs at me, but I know she works hard. She couldn't possibly do another job as well as this one because she couldn't find the time. I'd like to know when the baby is coming, but I decide not to ask in case Alan gets angry with me. I don't want him to get angry and jump on me like the bad boy did, even if it meant I'd get a lift home in Mr. Henderson's Mercedes.

When I walk into the main office, I'm relieved to see Melanie sitting at her desk. There doesn't seem to be a baby anywhere so it couldn't have been baby day after all.

"Hello Melanie," I say. "Were you sick yesterday? Are you okay now?"

"I'm fine Billy. Thank you for asking. I'm glad someone in this office gives a damn," she replies.

Now that Melanie is talking to me I don't want the conversation to end, so I try to think of something to say.

"I got a lift in Mr. Henderson's Mercedes," I offer. "He drove me home."

"I know Billy. That must have been very nice for you," she replies. "Some people are very lucky. They are very rich and they can buy anything they want. Then there are ordinary people like you and me who work hard every day and still can only dream about owning a fancy car or designer clothes."

"You wear lovely clothes Melanie and you're very pretty. If I had lots of money, I'd buy you a Mercedes like Mr. Henderson's," I offer.

"You are very sweet Billy," she says. "It's not people like Mr. Henderson who get up my nose. It's people like that stuck up old bitch, Mrs. Worthington. Do you know the woman I mean? She's got a face like a chewed toffee and she always has an expression like there's a bad smell under her nose. She was in the office the other day to sign her will."

"I know who she is," I reply. "I don't like her. My Aunty Mabel says she's a nasty piece of work."

"Your Aunty is a wise woman, Billy. That Mrs. Worthington is a nasty piece of work. When I was called in to Mr. Henderson's room to witness her will, she just carried on talking over me as if I wasn't there. She really is a bitch."

"What's a will, Melanie?" I ask.

"It's when you put down in writing what you want done with your belongings after you're dead," she says. "Most adults have them. Do you know what that old witch Worthington has done? She's cut all her relatives and friends out of her will and left all her worldly goods to some home for decrepit, senile, old men, but only if they erect a plaque on the wall renaming the place 'The Bella Worthington Memorial Centre'."

"Do you mean she's leaving them all her money? What about her house?" I ask.

"She's leaving everything to the charity, lock stock and barrel, including her house," she replies. "Have you ever heard anything so ridiculous? If I had her sort of money, I'd spend it on having fun. Why do the wrong people always get the money? She's the sort who'd probably win the lottery then moan that the prize money is too much."

I don't usually miss the chance to speak to Melanie because she's usually too busy to talk to me, but I need time to think about what she's told me.

"I have to go now Melanie," I say. "I need to get on with my deliveries. Betty will have them ready for me now. See you later."

What will my Aunty Mabel do if Mrs. Worthington gives her house away, I wonder? Where will she live? Aunty Mabel told my Mum she'd always have a home even if Mrs. Worthington died. She said she was going to be left the house. I think I'd better tell my Mum because she'll know what to do. She'll look after Aunty Mabel because they are best friends and best friends look after each other, just like I look after David. It's lucky Melanie told me about the will or Aunty Mabel wouldn't have found out until it was too late to make other plans. I love my Aunty Mabel and I hate Mrs. Worthington. I wish Aunty Mabel would find a nicer person to live with. Maybe she will now.

CHAPTER THIRTY-NINE

DAVID

There is a God. There is a God and he's smiling on me. Mark phoned. He telephoned me and said he misses me and he wants to talk things over. Thank you God, thank you Alexander Graham Bell for inventing the telephone.

I'm cleaning the flat as if my life depends on it. I don't want Mark to see any signs of despair. I don't want him to know how desperate I've been. I know I can make him want me again. I've prepared his favourite food and I've filled the flat with flowers. I've even bought new linen for the bed. There's champagne chilling in the fridge and Barbara Streisand is singing her heart out on the CD player. One single telephone call and I've gone from suicidal to full of hope. I'm so happy. I love him and he's coming back to me. With Mark at my side I'm king of the world.

The doorbell is ringing, he's early I think, almost twenty minutes early that's not like him.

"Coming," I shout as I take off my apron and throw it into the hall cupboard.

"Hello lover, I've missed you," I say, as I open the door.

"Hello David, I've brought a James Bond DVD," says Billy, as he enters the hall.

Billy, Christ I'd forgotten about him.

"You can't stay, Billy," I say. "I've got a visitor coming. He's going to arrive any minute."

He laughs, "That's a good joke, David," he says. "You had me going there. I'm the visitor. You invited me. Put the DVD in the machine please. I've got sweeties in my pocket. I bought toffees because they're your favourite." He thrusts his jacket at me.

"No Billy, I'm sorry," I insist. "Someone else is coming so I have to cancel us today. You'll have to leave. You'll have to leave now."

"I can't go home because my Mum is out and I haven't got a key," Billy says, stubbornly.

I don't need this Billy, I think, not now, anytime but now.

"Billy, I know you're disappointed, but you must leave," I insist.

I try to push him out of the door, but he's not going to be moved. He sits on the floor and folds his arms. We are both near to tears.

"I'm your best friend," he wails. "You've got to be nice to me because I'm your best friend. Your other visitor can watch James Bond too, I don't mind."

"Billy," I shout. "Get off the floor. You have to leave now, this minute. You're making me angry."

He begins to sob. Christ what will I do? I hear the close entrance door slam. It's Mark. Jesus Christ, what the hell will I do?

"Don't do this to me Billy. You're going to ruin my life. Get off the floor," I'm screaming at him.

"David is that you? Are you okay?" Mark calls.

"What's going on here? Who is this?" he asks nodding at Billy.

"I'm his best friend and I want to stay," Billy wails. "I was invited first and I've brought my film and sweets. I do lots of things for David. Secret things," he says, looking pointedly at me. "I don't want to leave."

"You seem to have your hands full," Mark says. "Maybe we should do this another time."

"No, don't leave," I beg. "I'll sort this out, please don't leave."

He stares at me. Please stay I pray.

"Okay," he says. "I'll pop round to the pub for half an hour. We'll talk when I get back."

"Thank you, thank you," I say. "I'll sort this mess. I'll fix everything. Oh, and don't eat anything. I've made all your favourite food and I've got champagne."

I hear the close entrance door slam as he leaves. I'm so angry with myself I punch the door. How pathetic I must have looked, pleading with him like that. I turn my attention to Billy.

"Shall we watch this now?" he says, getting to his feet and thrusting the disk in my face.

"You idiot, Billy," I snarl. "Don't you ever listen? Don't you understand English? I don't want you here. I want you to take your damned DVD and leave. I don't care where you go, just get out of here. Leave," I scream at him. "Get out and don't come back."

I watch him clamber down the stairs then I hear the entrance door close. I run to the window to check he's gone and I'm in time to see him wander into the road. My heart is in my mouth as a car screeches to a halt, missing him by inches.

"Idiot," I say under my breath, then immediately feel guilty. Of course he's an idiot, I think, he's retarded. He doesn't know any better. But I should know better. I should know better.

CHAPTER FORTY

BILLY

I'm so upset that I forget my Green Cross Code and a car nearly knocks me down. The driver opens the window and shouts. "Fucking idiot! Do you want to get killed?"

I can't stop crying because I've made David really angry and I don't think he wants to be my best friend any more. He didn't even want to see my James Bond DVD or eat the toffees I brought for him. I walk round the corner and sit on a wall. After a while, David's new best friend comes along the street. He sees me sitting on the wall but he crosses over so he doesn't have to walk past me. I don't want to stay here in case David comes out and shouts at me again, but I don't want to go home or I'll have to tell my Mum what has happened.

I cut through to Victoria Road and look in the shop windows, but because it is dinnertime all the shops are closed. David was meant to give me something to eat but it doesn't matter because I'm too upset to eat anything. I walk to the station and stand and watch the trains for a while, but it starts to rain and I'm bored. This station has two gates, one at the front, which opens onto Victoria Road and one at the back which is a mystery because I don't know where it goes. I decide to go out the back door and see where I end up.

When I walk through the back gate, I'm disappointed to see tenement flats and some storerooms. Nothing very exciting here, I think to myself. Then I notice lots of people going into one of the storerooms and I cross the road to have a look and see if I can tell what's inside. As I reach the door, a man wearing a hat opens it and says.

"In you come, Sir. Miserable night, isn't it?"

I wonder how he knows I'm miserable. When I go inside, the room is very busy. There's furniture all over the place. There are chairs piled on tables and desks and fridges and beds standing upended against the wall. I can see a big box with books and another with toys. Everything has a little white ticket with a different number stuck on it. People are lifting things out of boxes and looking at them then returning them to the boxes and a man is playing one of the pianos. There is a lovely big pram I'm sure Melanie would like for her baby and a box with DVDs which are mostly cartoons. I like cartoons.

Suddenly I hear a bang, bang, bang and I turn to see a man standing on a platform at the front of the room.

"Ladies and Gentlemen, if you'll please be quiet, we'll get started," he says. "May I remind you the terms are cash or cleared cheque before removal of goods. Lot numbers 22-27 are new and are subject to V.A.T. No smoking, talking or eating and that includes children, unless the child makes a noise in which case you have my permission to talk to them severely, smoke them or indeed eat them."

Everyone laughs but I don't understand the joke and I don't think making a joke about eating children is very funny.

"We'll do the small items first," he continues, "Starting with lot number one which is a Gentleman's gold pocket watch. Who'll start me at one hundred?"

Within a few minutes I think I understand what's going on. It seems to me the person who has his hand up at the right time, is the one who wins the item that the man in the brown apron is holding up. You have to guess the correct number then put your hand up when the man with the wooden hammer shouts it out. If you get it right, he asks you your name and the lady with the big book writes it down. I think it's a bit like Bingo.

The big pram is being shown now and I'd really like to win it for Melanie. The man has got to twenty-six and nobody has their hand up now.

"Is there any more?" he asks. "Are you all done?"

I put my hand up.

"Thank you, Sir, twenty eight. All done then at twenty-eight?"

Bang, he hits the desk with the wooden hammer.

"It's yours, Sir," he says. "Name please."

"Billy McDaid," I reply.

"Have you been here before, Mr. McDaid?" he asks.

I shake my head.

"Would you please give your name and address to the porter and leave a cash deposit," he says pointing to a man sitting at a desk near the front.

When I go over to the desk, I see the porter is the

same man who held the door open for me. I tell him my name and address and he asks me for a £10 deposit. I explain I've only got my emergency money.

"Don't worry Sir, I'll give you a receipt and when you've finished bidding, I'll return it when you settle up," he says.

"So I'll get my cash back?" I ask.

"Of course, Sir, no problem," he says and he smiles at me.

After a while, the box of DVDs are shown and I decide to try and win them for my Mum and me. I'm really excited because this is such good fun. When the man reaches forty-eight, I raise my hand, then the man says, "fifty" and bangs down the hammer.

"McDaid," he says to the lady with the big book. "Thank you, Sir," he says to me and I feel really important because he remembers my name.

By the time the clock on the wall says eight thirty I have managed to win lots of stuff and the competition is over. I'm not sure what to do next so I sit on one of the chairs and wait for everyone else to finish talking to the porter. When he is free, I go over to him.

"How are you paying Sir?" he asks.

I take out my receipt. "Can I have my £10 back now?" I ask.

"You have to write a cheque for £830 Sir," he says.

"But I don't have a cheque," I say. "I told you before that I only have my £10 emergency money and my bus ticket."

He looks at me for a moment or two then slaps his forehead.

"Oh fuck," he says. "Nigel, come over here. Quick," he shouts to the man with the hammer.

They speak to each other for a minute.

"Fucking Hell!" the man called Nigel says. "Didn't you realise he wasn't the full shilling when you took his details?"

"How could I?" the porter replies. "He told me his name and address and he gave me his deposit. Besides, he doesn't look like an eejit. I'm not a fucking psychologist. How the hell could I know?"

They both seem very angry and they keep talking to each other and looking at me. They are making me nervous. My Mum warned me about strangers and here I am stuck in a big storeroom with strangers. I feel frightened and I begin to cry. Maybe they'll lock me in. Maybe they're really bad men, like kidnappers.

"I want to go home," I cry. "I want my emergency money and I want to go home."

The man called Nigel opens a drawer in the desk and takes out a £10 note.

"Here," he says handing me the money. "Take it and get out of here. Don't come back. You've messed up everything."

I don't know what I've done, but everyone is angry with me so I run out of the door. I'm sorry they didn't give me my stuff after I won the competition, but at least I've got my money back and I've escaped from the kidnappers. I've had a terrible day. I've lost my best friend and I've nearly been captured by bad men.

I'm going home to my Mum. She'll look after me and she'll make me supper. My Mum always says a boy's best friend is his mum and she's right.

CHAPTER FORTY-ONE

MELANIE

He is a vision of rich elegance from his sleek black hair to his highly polished snakeskin shoes. My mother is fussing round him like a silly schoolgirl. I stand just outside the doorway watching. He is the epitome of sophistication. How proud I feel in my 'Versace' dress with my blonde hair and perfect figure accompanying this God to a different world from anything I've ever experienced before. Although my mother's front room is clean and freshly decorated, it suddenly seems shabby surroundings for beings such as us.

"Ah, there you are Melly," he says as I enter the room. "You look perfect. If you'll please excuse us Mrs. Coulson we really must be going now," he says, turning to my mother. "I must say it's clear to see where Melanie gets her good looks," he adds, flashing a pearly white smile at her. It's a corny line, but my mother has fallen for it hook, line and sinker. She actually blushes and she smiles coyly at him.

"What a lovely young man you are," she says. "I suppose you went to a private school," she says.

"Yes," he replies, smiling at me and winking. "My

parents thought it best. Now we really must go Melanie," he insists, and within minutes we have extricated ourselves from mother's clutches and we're in a taxi heading for the awards dinner.

"Now Melanie, there are some rules for tonight that you must observe," Jez says in a serious tone. "Firstly, you must not, under any circumstances, ask for anyone's autograph. These people cannot know you're in awe of them, even if you are. It doesn't matter who you see or how important they are or how impressed you are, no autographs, understand? Secondly, do not let anyone buy you a drink unless they're buying for both of us because I don't want anyone to get the wrong impression about you. Thirdly, and most importantly, no alcohol, if you do order a drink, make it a soft drink. We have to keep our wits about us if this is to work."

I sit nodding as Jez speaks because I don't want to upset him, but really, who the Hell does he think he is, lecturing me? He seems to forget he's a schoolboy and I'm a mature woman. I have plenty of experience with men and one or two of them were very wealthy. He goes on and on about moderation and decorum and how I should act. I think I'm perfectly capable of coping with a crappy dinner in a snobby hotel and I'm sure the odd glass of wine or two won't make a jot of difference. When I step through the door with this figure and hair and face, everyone will want to know who I am. Even Kate Moss would be jealous.

Finally, we arrive at the Hilton so I can escape from Jez's boring crap. I'm about to reach for the cab's door handle when a man in a monkey suit beats me to it.

"May I help you, Madam?" he asks, proffering his arm to support me.

"I can manage, thank you," I say abruptly.

I'm not some old lady or a drunk. I'm perfectly capable of getting out of a car myself. What a cheek, I think.

We enter the hotel through the automatic revolving door. The reception is very busy and I'm immediately surrounded by hordes of people. I'm surprised how huge and impersonal the place is. I'm wearing 'Versace' dammit, why is nobody looking at me?

"I want a drink Jez," I say. "Get me a Morgan's Spice and Coke please."

"I thought we agreed no alcohol," he replies. He stares at me pointedly. "Are you going to be all right? If this is too much for you to handle when we're hardly through the door, maybe we should leave now."

"Who the fuck do you think you're talking to, schoolboy? Just get me the damned drink and stop being a prick or they'll be no action tonight," I hiss at him.

I watch him stride to the bar and I feel very alone. Everybody seems to know everybody else but I don't know anyone except Jez. Gradually, I begin to recognise some famous faces from television and newspapers. They all seem much older and smaller in real life. I hear laughter from the group of women who are standing nearest to me and I'm about to smile at them when it dawns on me that I seem to be the focal point of their conversation. They're looking down their noses at me, snooty bitches. They all look like clones of each other. They're very elegant and their clothes are understated, muted colours with matching accessories. All are pencil thin and they have an air of confidence about them. They make me feel very uncomfortable and I wonder if their laughter is aimed directly at me. Is my dress too bright, too revealing or too sparkly? Am I too short, too young or too naive? What have I got myself into? I wish Jez would hurry up with my drink.

I look around for him but the place is so crowded. Two men with cameras are making their way towards me. I feel a buzz of excitement. They're probably here to photograph beautiful people for the media and they're coming over to me. Everything is okay. I feel confident again. I'm beautiful and these snooty bitches are has-beens.

"Here's your drink, Melly. The bar was packed," Jez says, as the photographers push past me, practically spinning me round in their rush to reach the snooty women.

I'm disappointed and overwhelmed with insecurities again.

Eventually, we go through to dinner and I find myself sitting at a table full of old farts. Jez has managed to sit me beside his father's friend, Gordo. He might be a footballer but he's an old man who hasn't played for two seasons. The speeches drone on and on and they're so dull I feel like slashing my wrists with boredom. Jez and Gordo talk about business and football and nothing else. I'm not included in the conversation. After an eternity, Jez gives me a wink. It's my cue to begin working on Gordo. I let my hand drift slowly up his thigh. I have finally become the centre of someone's attention.

After a moment or two, Jez excuses himself and leaves the table and Gordo immediately asks,

"Are you and young Jeremy an item?"

"Don't be daft," I reply. "He's only a boy. I'm just here to keep him out of mischief because he's using his father's tickets."

"Oh, do you know his father then?"

"Not really, but I wouldn't mind getting to know you," I reply, smiling and licking my lips suggestively. "I have a double room booked for tonight and Jez is going home. Would you care for a nightcap?"

He laughs and it has a dirty sound that makes my skin crawl. Just focus on the money I think to myself.

"Say Goodbye to the boy. Tell him you have a headache and give me the room number. I'll be up in half an hour and I'll bring some booze," he replies, wasting no time on niceties.

I haven't lost my touch, he is obviously gagging for it. This will be easier than I thought.

I arrange with Jez that he'll say his goodbyes to Gordo and me, but remain in the hotel until he's sure I'm safe. Once he disappears out of sight, I go to the room to wait for Gordo. It doesn't take long for him to arrive and he wastes no time in getting into bed.

"Right sweetheart," he says. "We both know why we're here. Come to bed my little peach."

Little peach, where did that line come from?

Gordo wants the lights left on. Gordo wants me on the top. Gordo wants me to say, "Fuck me Daddy. Fuck me hard." Gordo is a prick but he's a prick with lots of money, so Gordo gets what Gordo wants.

Suddenly there is a bright flash of light. I'm about to say, 'What was that?' when I'm pushed roughly off

Gordo and I find myself in a heap on the floor beside the bed.

"What the fuck's your game, Jeremy?" Gordo yells.

"What's going on?" I manage to say.

Jez is standing at the foot of the bed with a camera and he is snapping photograph after photograph.

"Come here you wee bastard. Give me that fucking camera," Gordo shouts, and he practically flies off the bed. Jez makes a run for it and Gordo follows until he realises he's in the hotel corridor and is naked. He storms back into the room, his face like thunder.

"Did you know about this?" he asks, screaming into my face. "Is this something the pair of you planned?"

I am so stunned and frightened I can only cry. He grabs me roughly by the arm and pulls me to my feet.

"Speak to me," he yells. "I want answers now. How did he get in? How did he get a key? What exactly is going on?"

"Jez booked the room," I say between sobs. He just gave me one key. I didn't know there was anything wrong, but he must have had a second key that he kept for himself. I didn't expect anything like this to happen," I say truthfully. "Maybe he thought I'd be here on my own."

"Oh Jesus, sweet Jesus," Gordo says with a sigh. "That's it, of course that's it. The stupid boy thought you'd be here on your own. He was probably trying to get some nude shots of you to show his pals and he got more than he bargained for. I'm sorry for yelling at you sweetheart. I probably scared the shit out of him and that's why he bolted."

I am beginning to feel calmer now Gordo has stopped shouting at me, but at this precise moment, I could kill Jez. What the hell is he playing at I wonder? This isn't what we planned.

"You understand I must leave now, Melanie," Gordo says. "I'll speak to Jeremy in the morning and sort this mess out. I'm sorry our night of passion didn't quite work out as we'd planned."

It takes him a couple of minutes to dress then he leaves, taking the booze he brought with him.

I am completely drained. I don't want to stay in this room a moment longer and I don't want to hang about this hotel, so I quickly change into my spare clothes and pack my borrowed dress into my overnight bag than make my way downstairs to the lobby. There is no sign of Jez and I feel conspicuous amongst the rich and famous when I'm dressed in jeans and a sweater, so I discreetly exit to look for a taxi.

"Goodbye Madam, I hope you had a nice evening," the doorman says as I leave.

He smiles knowingly at me and I'm sure he thinks I'm some kind of high-class hooker. My cheeks are burning with embarrassment and I'd like to punch the smug bastard's lights out.

CHAPTER FORTY-TWO

JEZ

What a rush, what a fantastic rush, it's better than drugs, better than sex. I am whooping with the buzz, completely wired and skipping down the hallway. I did it. I fucking did it. Perfection, everything went like clockwork. I am the master. I am a fucking genius. I bet Melanie is a bit pissed off at the moment but too bad. Too fucking bad. I couldn't tell her my plans or she might have blown everything. She'll get over it when I tell her she's going to make a grand for a few hours work. That should keep her sweet.

Any newspaper will pay at least six grand for these negatives. Gordo's not short of money, in fact he's rolling in it, so who knows what I might get when the bidding starts. I'll give Gordo first refusal, at the right price of course. After all, he is my father's friend, even if he is an arse.

I feel like shouting at the top of my voice because I'm so elated. I'm so good. I'm the greatest. This will make me seriously rich. With careful planning I'll be able to pull this sort of scam over and over again. I'll be able to pay off the boys when they get out of jail. I'm going up in the world and I'll never need to mix with scum again.

CHAPTER FORTY-THREE

BILLY

My Mum is annoyed because I won't go to church with her this morning. I've told her I've got other plans.

"Other plans, hmph!" she says. "Nothing and no-one is more important than God. What are you going to do that's so urgent?"

I don't want to tell her so I look at the ground and say nothing. If she doesn't look into my eyes, she won't see the truth and it gives me time to think of a lie.

"I'm waiting, Billy," she persists.

I continue staring at the ground.

"Oh, I haven't time for this nonsense," she says. "Just make sure you're back here at five o'clock because Aunty Mabel is coming round for dinner."

I keep staring at the ground until I hear the front door slam then I know she's left.

I'm pleased Aunty Mabel is visiting because my Mum said she has a present for me. She told me Aunty Mabel was very pleased to hear about Mrs. Worthington's will because it let her make plans for her future. I wonder what present she'll bring me, maybe she'll bring sweets. I like sweets.

I hadn't really planned to go anywhere in particular today, I just wanted to spend some time on my own, without Mum. I've been thinking and thinking until my head hurts, trying to work out why David wants his new best friend instead of me. I finally decide it must be because he has black hair. David has black hair and his new best friend has black hair, even Jez has black hair, but I have yellow hair. Melanie has yellow hair and she's pretty and she has lots of friends so I suppose yellow hair is okay if you're a girl. Now I know what my problem is I can do something to make it right.

I know you can change your hair colour with hair dye because my Mum uses it and they talk about it in adverts on the telly, but I don't know where you get it and it smells bad and it makes your eyes sting. When my black shoes went white in the rain, my Mum made them black again with shoe polish. Shoe polish smells nice and I know we have some in the kitchen cupboard so I go and fetch it.

I take the tin of polish and the little brush to the bathroom so I can look in the mirror and I carefully brush some onto my hair. It's a bit sticky, like black hair gel, but it looks great and it makes my hair completely black. When I'm finished, I put the polish back in the cupboard. I'm so excited about my black hair that I decide to visit David so I can show him right away. I'm sure when he's sees me he'll want me to be his best friend again. I get my coat and my new bus-pass and run to the bus stop.

The people on the bus keep staring at me. It's probably because I look so cool with my black hair. I like it when people notice me and I smile at them. Some of the people smile back at me. This makes me feel happy because people don't usually smile at me on the bus. I'm quite sorry to get off the bus at the stop, but I soon see people in the street are looking at me too, so I smile and wave at them as I walk to David's house. When I arrive, I run up the stairs to his flat and ring the doorbell, then I cross my fingers and hope he's at home. I can't wait to see the look on his face when he sees my black hair.

CHAPTER FORTY-FOUR

DAVID

I'm struggling with pots and pans of steaming food trying to create a culinary masterpiece in the kitchen when the doorbell rings. I'm already short of at least one pair of hands so I call out to Mark, who is reading the Sunday papers.

"Would you answer the door please, my hands are full."

"It won't be for me," he replies irritably.

I hear him sigh, throw down his paper and walk to the door. Some things never change, I think. He is still as selfish and lazy as ever. However, I would much rather have him here with his flaws and faults than be on my own again.

"David," he calls. "You'd better come to the door."

"Who is it?" I call back. "Can't you bring them in?"

"No, David. Come to the door right now. Hurry up."

His voice sounds a bit panicky so I turn everything on the stove off and do as I'm asked. I can't believe my eyes at the sight that awaits me.

"Hi, David," Billy says. "What do you think?

Tarah!" he sings, holding his arms out like a jazz singer.

"I've got black hair now, just like you."

Mark and I stare incredulously at the sight before us. Billy's hair is covered in something black and sticky. It is sticking up in lumpy, glutinous clumps all over his head. His ears are black and long streaks of the substance have run down his face and under his chin. He looks like a tar baby.

"What have you done, Billy?" I ask. "What is that stuff?"

I pray it isn't anything out of a garden or a drain.

"It's shoe polish. Isn't it great? I'll be just like him now," he says, pointing at Mark. "I'll be able to be your best friend again. It looks cool, doesn't it?"

"I can't leave him like this," I say to Mark. "Will you help me, please?"

"Oh no," he says holding his hands defensively in front of him. "He's all yours. You're on your own. I'll be reading the papers. Oh, and don't get any of that goop on my stuff."

I lead Billy to the bathroom and help him to remove his coat and his shirt. Then I have him kneel on the floor and lean over the bath so I can use the shower to wash his hair. It takes me over an hour and a whole bottle of shampoo before I'm sure all the shoe polish is off. Then I take him into the lounge and make us all some tea. I know I haven't been fair to Billy and I try to explain to him as gently as I can that he and I are still friends, but Mark and I are family. I explain to him that this is Mark's home and he's moving back in with me. He sits in silence, listening to my every word, then without warning he turns on Mark.

"You made David cry," he accuses him. "You left him on his own and he was very sad. I looked after David and kept him from being lonely. I gave him special massages even though Mr. Henderson said it was wrong. I was his best friend and you're a nasty piece of work."

I am horrified. Mark rounds on me.

"What special massage? What the fuck is he talking about? Have you been messing with this geek?"

I sit in shocked silence, numbed and sickened. Mark's face is white with rage and disbelief.

"Answer me David. What's been going on?"

Billy looks very scared.

"I'm sorry I told," he wails. "I'm sorry I told the secret. I'm going home now. I'll see you another time." He lifts his coat and heads out of the door.

I sit with my head in my hands as my whole world crashes around me.

"It's not like you think," I begin to say. "I can explain. It's not like you think."

"It is exactly like I think. No matter what fiction you concoct," Mark spits at me. "Whatever way you try to turn or twist this, it will still be the same. You fucked a geek. You took advantage of a retard. You are garbage. I was only away for a few weeks to get my head together. What kind of sick freak are you?"

I can't answer him. I'm too distraught. Everything he says is true.

"We're through, you and me," he continues. "You know this means we're through?"

"No, Mark, please," I beg. "We can work this out. I'm sure we can work this out."

He looks at me and his eyes are filled with disgust.

"We can never work this out, David. NEVER. Don't you see what you've done? He's like a child. It's like fucking with a child."

I cannot answer. I'm shocked by the reality of his words. I'm losing the love of my life because I can't keep my dick in my pants. I'm losing the love of my life because of Billy.

CHAPTER FORTY-FIVE

BILLY

David's friend, Mark was very angry, but I don't care. I'm pleased he was angry because he'll probably go away then David will want me back. I'll be his best friend again. We'll watch films together and eat sweets and he'll call me his 'Sweet Billy Boy'. I'm pleased I don't need to have black hair. It was great when all those people noticed me and waved at me but it made my head feel hot and itchy.

I'm not sure what the time is and I can't wait to see the present Aunty Mabel has bought me, so I run to catch the bus for home. When I arrive, Mum and Aunty Mabel are in the lounge.

"Hello, Son," Mum says. "Have you had any lunch?"

"What have you brought me Aunty Mabel? I ask. "Where's my present?"

"That's not very polite, Billy," Mum says. "You haven't even taken off your coat or said hello to us."

I throw my coat over a chair.

"Hello Mum, hello Aunty Mabel. Where's my present?"

"Where are your manners, Billy?" Mum scolds. "I'm sorry Mabel, he's over excited."

"That's okay, here's your present, Pet. You did me a very good turn, Billy. You certainly kept your eye on Mrs. Worthington. You're a real hero in my book."

She turns to Mum. "I'm going to tackle the old witch when I get home. I'm not going to let her treat me like a fool any longer."

"Remember, you can move in here with us for a while if things don't work out, Mabel," Mum says.

"Thank you, Dear, that gives me strength," Aunty Mabel replies.

"Wow!" I say as I rip off the wrapping paper. "Three presents, look Mum, a book with pictures of James Bond, a James Bond DVD that I haven't seen yet and a box of chocolates. Thank you, Aunty Mabel. Thank you very, very much."

"You're welcome, Pet. You're more than welcome."

This is turning into a really great day. David will soon be my best friend again. Aunty Mabel has given me three presents and she says I'm a hero and Mum has made my favourite dinner with chocolate cake for dessert. I bet even James Bond isn't as happy as this.

CHAPTER FORTY-SIX

BELLA

The church service was so inspiring today. The Minister's sermon could have been written especially with me in mind. He preached about charity and how it's better to give than to receive and also about how we come into this world with nothing and exit with nothing. He said those who die leaving nothing behind but the memories of good and charitable deeds are the ones remembered by others and, are therefore, truly blessed. That describes me to a tee. I will be remembered for my charitable deed, especially when they erect a plaque with my name on it and re-name the building 'The Bella Worthington Memorial Hall'. Yes, God will surely welcome me with open arms. He's probably preparing my wings right now. There is, no doubt, a special place in heaven for the likes of me. Who knows, in the next world I might even be rubbing shoulders with Mother Theresa or Gandhi, unless of course they have a separate section for foreigners. I suppose one does get one's rewards in heaven. I have to rub shoulders with some very common people here on earth. Now that I've secured my place in heaven, I think I'll stop doing a share of the hospital visiting. It's such a depressing job and sick people are so smelly and boring. Besides, I might catch something. I'd rather have a few more years here on earth, even if the next world is a better place and has a better class of neighbour.

I told Mrs. Jamieson about the donation I've left in my will. I know she won't blab to all and sundry, she can keep a secret because her father was a former Lord Provost. She was very impressed.

"Bella," she said. "This sermon could have been written about you. Well done, Dear."

She called me 'Dear' then she invited me to tea with the 'League of Genteel Ladies' next Tuesday afternoon. We're going to discuss a fundraiser for the widows of the parish. That is to say, the genteel, widows of the parish and not the lower classes, because the lower classes don't need our help. They're used to poverty.

Before I know it, the clock in the hall strikes the hour of eight. My, my, how quickly time passes when you're enjoying yourself. I hear Mabel's key in the lock. Good, I think to myself, she's home in time to make me a hot drink before I retire to my room.

"Hello Mabel," I call, when I hear the front door close. "Put the kettle on, Dear and we'll have a nice cup of tea."

"Very well, Bella," she replies. "I have something important I wish to discuss with you and I think we'll both benefit from a cup."

I don't like the sound of that. I do hope she's not going to spoil my good day with her petty problems. She brings in the tea and sits facing me.

"I'll get straight to the point, Bella," she begins. "I want a pay rise."

"But Mabel," I protest. "You know I scrimp and save in order to cover your wages. I'm not a rich woman. Besides, I've already told you you'll get this house if I die first."

"Rubbish," she says. "I know that's not true. I know this house is being left to charity."

I am flabbergasted. "What do you mean?" I splutter. "Who told you that?"

"Never mind who told me, you can't deny it."

I look at the determined set of her jaw and I know I'm beaten.

"If I don't get my raise," she continues. "Then I'm afraid you'll just have to find another housekeeper."

"But Mabel, Dear," I protest. "You are more than just a housekeeper you're my companion, my friend."

"I'm so glad you feel that way, Bella because I'd like a raise of forty pounds a week, beginning immediately. I also want security of tenure in this house until I die or have to go into a home. The charity will still get the house, but this way they won't be able to turf me out into the street if you die first."

I think about what she's said. I suppose it will do me no harm to give her security of tenure. In fact, it would show me in a good light as a benevolent employer. There is room for negotiation here, I decide.

"I will want a letter from your solicitor confirming the security of tenure and stating he will advise me immediately should the circumstances of your will change," Mabel says.

"You seem to have thought of everything, Mabel," I say, bitterly. "But where would you go if I can't comply?"

"You mean if you won't comply," she says. "I have

another offer and I'll move out on Friday if I don't hear from your solicitor by then."

She has me over a barrel and she knows it. I play my hand as convincingly as I can.

"I'll agree to the security of tenure, but only if you accept a raise of just fifteen pounds a week as that's all that I can afford. Take it or leave it," I say.

"I'll take it," she says. "I'm glad that's settled, Bella. I believe in clearing the air."

I feel tired and drained.

"I'm going to retire now, Mabel because I'm very tired. Please wake me at nine-thirty with my breakfast," I say. I have to re-establish my position as the one who is in charge.

"Of course, Bella, goodnight and sleep well," she replies.

But I don't have a good night and I don't sleep well. Someone has betrayed my confidence. It couldn't have been Mrs. Jamieson because there hasn't been enough time for it to get back to Mabel. It must have come from Henderson's. The only connection I can make is the idiot son of Mabel's friend but he only delivers mail for Mr. Henderson, he couldn't possibly have seen my private file, unless of course someone who has access to the file has spoken to him. During the war there was a saying 'loose talk costs lives'. This is a case of loose talk costing me money. I'll get to the bottom of this and someone will pay for their indiscretion. I'll make sure of it.

CHAPTER FORTY-SEVEN

BILLY

It is nearly Halloween. The Railway Club that my Aunty Mabel is a member of is holding a party for special people and I'm invited. I'll be able to dress up and play games like 'dooking for apples' and I'll get lots of sweets and nuts and fruit. I had a great time last year. I hope my friend Craig is there because he's always in my team for the games. Mum says he's a bit slow because he has something called 'Down Syndrome', but I don't think he's slow, in fact he's one of the fastest runners in my team. With Craig in my team we'll win all the prizes. If this 'Down Syndrome' thing makes him slower, just think how fast he'd be if he didn't have it. He could probably win a gold medal or the world cup or something like that.

I've decided to dress up as a monster this year and I've seen a really cool mask which has a green face and bolts coming out of the neck. I'll be able to run after the girls and frighten them and they'll scream and run away and Craig and I will laugh and laugh. Mum has given me money to buy the mask and I'm going to the shop after I make my next delivery.

They seem to take ages to sign for their letter at

Wilsons but finally I get away and I manage to buy my mask. I'm almost back at the office to pick up my afternoon deliveries when I meet Jez.

"Hello Billy," he says. "I was hoping to bump into you. Could you do a wee job for me?"

I'm really happy to see Jez and I show him my mask.

"It's cool isn't it, Jez? I'm going to wear it to frighten the girls."

"I don't think you'll need a mask for that, big man," he says, laughing. "You're scary enough without it. Will you please concentrate on what I have to say, Billy," he continues, "Because it's very important. I have a special mission for you. Do you think you can handle it?"

"I think so," I reply. "My Aunty Mabel thinks I'm a hero."

"Well then, you're just the man for the job. I want you to deliver this envelope to Melanie. It has photographs in it so you mustn't bend it. Give it to her before work finishes today and tell her she's to keep them safe and I have the negatives. Do you understand?"

I nod my head and repeat what he's said.

"I've to tell Melanie these are secret photos and Jez has the negatives and she's to keep them safe."

"Close enough, good man Billy," he says. "Now put them in your case and keep them safe."

This is exciting I think, just like James Bond.

"I'd give them to her myself, but she's out for lunch and I don't want to hang around in case I bump into my Uncle Peter so you're doing me a favour."

He gives me a pound for sweets and then he leaves.

Melanie doesn't come back after lunch in time for me to give her the envelope and I have to start my afternoon deliveries, so I keep it safely stashed in my case and I can give it to her at the end of the day. I keep repeating the message to myself so I remember to tell her exactly what Jez has said. It's exciting knowing I have secret photos in my bag. I wonder if Jez is a spy. Maybe he is the real James Bond and Melanie is Miss Moneypenny.

CHAPTER FORTY-EIGHT

MELANIE

I got such a shock when Jez burst into the bedroom and Gordo went ballistic. I had no idea he was going to do that. I travelled home in the taxi, crying my eyes out. It was lucky Mum had already gone to bed or I'd have had some explaining to do. Anyway, once I telephoned Jez he explained everything. He said he didn't tell me anything in case I inadvertently blurted something out and gave the game away. Jez said if Gordo thought I was up to something he might have become very nasty. Jez was simply protecting me. He told me we're each going to get a thousand pounds. A whole thousand pounds for a few hours work, I got a free dinner into the bargain and Jez said I could keep the Versace dress. He bought it for me on his mother's credit card, as a little bonus. I'm into the big time now. I'm finished with off the peg clothes and I'm finished with off the peg boyfriends, I want designer all the way.

I'm going to be a bit late getting back to the office after lunch because I simply had to go back to Versace to check out a scarf I saw the other day. The assistant couldn't have been more attentive. She said she was delighted I've decided to keep the dress because it looked so good on me. Then she asked me all about the Awards Dinner and I told her these things aren't all they're cracked up to be and are really rather dull. She even made me a cup of coffee while I looked at the scarves. What a difference it makes when you have a bit of class. Oh God, I'm actually twenty minutes late for work. Alan will be a bit miffed, but the wimp won't say anything, he wouldn't dare because he's scared of Jez.

"Where have you been?" Alan hisses at me when I step through the door.

"Don't get your knickers in a twist, I'm only a few minutes late," I reply.

"Twenty minutes, you are twenty minutes late and the boss wants to see you."

"Mr. Henderson wants to see me, whatever for, surely not because I'm a few minutes late?"

"I have no idea why he wants you, but I've been making excuses for you for the last twenty minutes, so get a move on."

When I knock on Mr. Henderson's door, Margaret his secretary opens it.

"Take a seat for a minute," she says, pointing to a straight-backed chair just outside the door. "Mr. Henderson will be ready for you shortly."

She goes back into his office and closes the door and I sit twiddling my thumbs for fifteen minutes before I'm called into the room. Mr. Henderson is seated behind the desk and Margaret is on his right, there's a chair at the front of the desk and Margaret gestures for me to sit down. This seems a bit formal, I think.

"A serious complaint has arisen, Melanie, and I

have to fully investigate it. That's the reason Margaret is here, to take precise notes," he says.

"A complaint," I say. "What am I supposed to have done?"

"Don't get upset, Melanie," he replies. "I don't know if you've done anything yet, I'm simply investigating the complaint. I'd like to ask you one or two questions regarding Mrs. Worthington's will. That was the will I asked you to witness last week. Do you remember?"

"Yes," I reply. "I remember witnessing it. Did I sign the wrong part or something?" I'm beginning to feel quite uneasy.

"Did you discuss the content of the will with anyone outside of this office?" he asks.

"No, of course not," I reply. "I never discuss my work outside of the office. I know everything is confidential."

"Could you have mentioned the will to anyone inside the office? Maybe one of the other girls?"

I think back to that day and a wave of fear passes over me. Oh my God, I think, I did mention the will. I told Billy about it but surely he doesn't count, he's got mashed potato for brains.

"You've become rather pale, Melanie," Mr. Henderson says. "Are you all right? Is there something you want to tell me?"

"I did mention it," I admit. "But I just said something in passing to Billy. It wouldn't have meant anything to him."

"You do know any mention of the content of confidential papers in or out of this office constitutes gross misconduct. You are aware of that, are you not?" he asks.

I'm feeling very nervous and slightly sick.

"Will you please answer my question, Melanie?"

"Y yes," I stammer. "I am aware of that. But surely Billy doesn't count, he wouldn't understand the significance of what I said."

"On the contrary, Miss Coulson, Billy would understand exactly the significance of what you said. Are you aware that Billy's aunt is Mrs. Worthington's housekeeper?"

Tears fill my eyes and threaten to overflow at any moment. I bite my lip and try to control myself. Mr. Henderson stares at me, unblinking.

"No, I didn't think so," he says. "Under the circumstances I have no alternative than to suspend you until further notice. You will be paid during your suspension, but you must not step foot in the office until the investigation into this matter is complete and a decision is made about how the matter will be handled. Do you understand what I've said?"

I nod my head. I cannot speak. I am distraught. I might lose my job because of Billy. I might lose my job because of an idiot with mashed potato for brains.

CHAPTER FORTY-NINE

BILLY

My case is empty apart from the envelope for Melanie. I'm not sure what to do because everyone has left the office. They all walked past me and said 'Goodnight', everyone except Melanie. I wonder if maybe she's in the ladies' toilet, but I can't go in to check because it's not allowed.

"Why are you still here, Billy?" Mr. Henderson asks, as he comes out of his room. "Everyone has gone home and I'm about to lock up."

"I've got to see Melanie," I reply. "I've got something for her."

"She had to leave early today and it's unlikely that she'll be back in the office this week. Is it something important?"

"It's very important," I reply. "They're secret photos in an envelope from Jez. I'm on a special mission."

"Let me see the envelope," he says.

I take it from my case and hand it to him.

"And this is from Jez to Melanie you say?"

"Yes," I reply. "He gave it to me and said I was to

tell Melanie he has the negatives and she's to keep these safe. I think Jez is a spy like James Bond," I add.

"Well then Billy, as it's so important, why don't I sign for this and I'll see Melanie gets it. Then you can run and catch your bus."

"But I don't have anything for you to sign," I say. "It's not on my sheet."

"Give me the sheet and I'll add it to it," he says, smiling at me. "I can do that you know because I'm the boss."

I'm so pleased Mr. Henderson is going to take the envelope for me because I don't know where Melanie is and Jez might be angry if I take it to her house.

Now I've completed all my deliveries, I can go home. I'm relieved my special mission is sorted out. I could be a spy's assistant. I'm sure every spy has an assistant to help them with things. I could make telephone calls and deliver secret messages and wear disguises so baddies don't know who I am. It would be very exciting and I've already had some practice, delivering secret messages.

I decide to get some practice at wearing disguises so I put on my monster mask to travel home. When I get to the bus stop, Mrs. Worthington is there. I don't like her and I usually keep out of her way, but because I'm in disguise, I stand right beside her.

"Get away from me, you horrible creature," she shouts. "Get away, before I call someone in authority."

She doesn't know it's me. She called me a horrible creature so she must think I'm really a green-faced monster. It makes me laugh and laugh. I think I'll be a spy instead of a superhero because spies have so much fun.

CHAPTER FIFTY

JEZ

I think my uncle has finally flipped his lid. First, he wants me to stay in school all day then I get called out of class half way through the afternoon and told to go straight to his office. I wish he'd make up his fucking mind, silly old bastard. I wonder why the great man has summoned me. I don't suppose it's to pat me on the back and congratulate me, no, that would never happen.

When I arrive at Uncle's office, Margaret the secretary shows me straight to his room. Well deary, deary me, I think, the old bastard is rather upset. His face is white with rage and his hands are balled into fists, his lips are being pressed so tightly together, they've formed a single angry line. Someone has upset him big time and I suspect that someone is me.

"Hello Uncle," I say, extending my hand for him to shake. "How lovely to see you. Are we having tea?"

"Sit down, Jeremy," he hisses through clenched teeth. "I already know you're a smart-arsed little prick, no reason to prove it."

He has never spoken to me like that, something is

seriously wrong. I sit down quickly and silently and try to avoid staring at his angry face.

"You've been a nasty little shit, haven't you Jeremy? A very nasty little shit," he snarls. "Do you want to tell me about it?"

Put my own head on the block, not likely I think.

"I don't know what you're talking about, Uncle," I reply. "You're obviously upset. Could it be something you ate?"

"You think you're so clever, don't you Jeremy? But then you've never been to jail. You can't imagine what it would be like to be stuck in a cell for twenty hours a day, trapped there with some body builder who takes a shine to the pretty, new boy, can you Jeremy?"

He's leaning over the desk and is screaming into my face. His spit lands on my cheek, but I resist the temptation to wipe it away.

"No Uncle, you're right, I can't imagine it," I reply, smiling. "But I'm sure you could enlighten me."

His hand grabs my shoulder and for a moment I think he's going to lose control and hit me. I tense my body in anticipation of the blow. I think he shocks himself because he suddenly releases me and sinks back into his chair. He seems to shrink in front of my eyes as if he's spent.

"Tell me about Gordo Fernie," he says. His hands cover his face and his elbows are resting on the desk. He looks exhausted.

"He's a friend of Father's," I offer.

"I spoke to him earlier today," he continues. "He was extremely upset. He told me you're trying to extort money from him. I advised him to go to the police."

"You told him what?" I splutter. "He's talking rubbish. It's his word against mine. He has no proof. The police would send him away with a flea in his ear."

"So you don't deny it then. You have been trying to blackmail him," he says.

"You tell me, Uncle, you seem to have all the answers."

He throws a familiar looking envelope onto the desk. The photos, bloody hell, somehow he has the photos.

"I believe you took these, Jeremy. Gordo Fernie and an unknown blonde, except the blonde isn't unknown, Jeremy, is she?"

I have run out of smart remarks. All I can think of is my money getting further and further away from me.

"I've managed to calm Gordo down," he continues. "By assuring him I will personally deliver the negatives to him today. If you don't give them to me, along with any copies you've made, I will have no choice but to give these photos to the police. Do I make myself absolutely clear?"

"Like crystal," I reply.

I lift the negatives out of my inside pocket and throw them onto the desk.

"I guess we have nothing more to say then," I say, and I stand and turn to leave. The office feels claustrophobic and I can't wait to get outside into the air.

"I'm not finished yet," he shouts. "You won't leave until I tell you to."

"Or what?" I ask. "What can an old fart like you possibly do to me? Cut me out of your will perhaps? So what, I can earn my own money, I don't need yours. Next week I shall become eighteen, legally an adult. I don't need dear Mater and Pater. I don't need money and I certainly don't need you. You'd better be careful, Uncle," I threaten. "Better make sure I'm not mentioned in your will. Who knows what a hard-nosed bastard like me is capable of, better watch your back, Uncle," I say as a parting shot.

His face is as red as a beetroot and he looks as if he might have a seizure. I storm out of the office, slapping Margaret soundly on the bottom as I pass her in the corridor. I am free, I think. Finally, I am free.

I am so angry at losing my money. It's all I can think about. Why on earth did Billy give him those photos? I've lost a small fortune and it's all Billy's fault.

CHAPTER FIFTY-ONE

BILLY

Tomorrow night is Guy Fawkes Night and I'm going to a fireworks display at Clarkston Rugby Club. They hold it every year and every year I get sparklers and a hot dog. I like the bonfire. I like the way it sparks and pops and crackles. Mum doesn't let me have matches, she says they're dangerous. If I was allowed matches, I would build the biggest bonfire in the world in our back garden and I would put a guy right on the top of it and watch it burn.

When I leave the office, I see some boys dragging a guy in a cart up and down the street. They are stopping people and asking them for money for the guy. I don't understand why the people are giving them money because a guy isn't a real person and only real people can spend money. As I make my way to the bus stop, I see lots of shops displaying firework posters in their windows. Some little boys come running out of one of the shops, they're very excited and they're talking loudly and laughing. One of the boys takes a box of matches out of his pocket and they all stand in a huddle as he lights something one of the other boys is holding. Then the second boy throws what he's holding into the shop. There is a loud bang, bang, bang, bang sound. The boys shriek with laughter and a man comes running out of the shop.

"Fuck you, you little fuckers. Fuck you," he shouts.

"Fuck yourself," the boys shout back and then they run away, laughing.

When the man goes back into the shop, I carry on walking along the street

I wish I was allowed matches.

I'm thinking about all the fun I'll have at the firework display when suddenly I'm pushed into a lane behind a row of flats. Voices are shouting in my ears and I'm being dragged and pushed, kicked and punched into the place where the big bins are kept behind the flats. Oh no, it's the bad boys. I'm frightened the bad boys have got me.

"Hello, moron. Have you missed me?" the first boy says.

"No," I say. "Let me go. I want to go home. I'll miss my bus."

"You've been a very naughty boy," the biggest one says.

"We're going to teach you a lesson you won't forget," says the third.

"First you're going to tell us where Jez is. We can't seem to find him, even though he told big Tam here he had our money."

"I don't know where he is," I lie.

I know he's usually at the bus stop at this time of day, but I'm not going to tell them.

"That's a real shame." Tam says. "Because if you don't know where he is, he won't be able to help you, will he?"

I say nothing. I stand with my arms wrapped round my head to try to protect myself from their punches. The boy with a tattoo on his head is holding a big can in his hand. He unscrews the lid of the can and splashes liquid from the can all over me. It smells funny and the smell makes my eyes cry and my head feel dizzy.

"Stop," I cry. "You're making me all wet. Stop. That stuff smells bad."

Big Tam takes some matches from his pocket. "You caused my friends here to go to jail," he says. "The wet stuff you're wearing is petrol and the only thing keeping me from turning you into a Roman candle is that Jez said he has our money. Now tell me where he is."

I'm really frightened. I know what happens when you set fire to petrol with matches because I've seen it in films. I've got to get away, I think, I've got to get away now. I punch the boy who is holding the matches in the stomach, just like I've seen James Bond punch. He doubles up and falls to the ground then I push one of the others hard and he falls over too. The third boy backs away from me and I run and I run until I'm back on the main road. Then I walk quickly to the bus stop. The smell of the petrol is making me very dizzy.

I see Mrs. Worthington at the stop and I stagger towards her.

"Help me, please help me. The bad boys are coming and they've got matches," I say. "You can arrest them because you're a lady soldier." I tug at her sleeve. "Please help me."

"Get away from me," she shouts, and pushes me roughly. "Get away from me you disgusting creature."

I turn and almost fall because the petrol fumes are making me so dizzy. I manage to grab hold of the next person in the queue and try to steady myself. My hands manage to grab him round the waist and as I slowly slide to my knees, I look up at his face and I see it is David.

"Help me, David," I beg. "The bad boys are coming. Please help me."

"Get back, don't touch me," he says pushing my hands away. "I don't know you anymore. Go away."

I fall onto my back and I lie on the ground. When I look up, I'm looking into the prettiest face in the whole world. It's Melanie.

"Please help me, Melanie," I plead. "They're coming to get me."

She folds her arms and glowers at me.

"Good," she says. "It's about time someone made you pay for the misery you've caused."

I turn my eyes towards Jez, who is standing beside her.

"They're looking for you, Jez," I say. "But I didn't tell them anything so they don't know where you are. Please don't let them hurt me," I beg.

"So you didn't tell them anything," he repeats. "That's a first. If you had just kept your big mouth shut, Melanie and I would be rolling in money."

"And I would still have Mark in my life," David says.

"And I would still have control of my money," Mrs. Worthington adds.

"But I've been helping," I cry. "I've been keeping an eye on you all."

"No, you've been meddling," Mrs. Worthington says.

"Spoiling everything," says David.

"Destroying everything we've worked for," adds Melanie.

"You're a waste of space," Jez says.

"But I'm a hero," I cry, "A hero."

"No you're not, you're a retard," Jez shouts.

No one moves. They all stare down at me. I manage to struggle to my feet.

"You're just like the bad boys," I say. "You want me gone. You want me to burn up and die."

Nobody disagrees, their angry faces glare at me.

"If I was allowed matches I'd light one right now then you'd all be sorry," I say. "If my Mum allowed me to have matches, I'd do it, I really would."

Jez smiles to himself, fishes about in his pocket then produces something that he holds out towards me.

"Here," he says laughing. "Have my safety lighter. I'm sure your Mum would allow you to have that. Take it," he snarls. "Put us all out of our misery."

I reach over and take the lighter then look at their angry faces. I was trying to help them, trying to put things right and they all hate me. None of them will help me. I hold the lighter at arm's length and scan their faces again. Will no one help me? I run my finger over the switch. It makes a satisfying 'click' but it doesn't light. If I keep the lighter at arm's length away from me, away from the petrol, I won't get hurt, but I might give them a fright. The lighter clicks again. David's expression changes, his mouth opens and he holds his hands up in front of him as if he is trying to stop something.

"No, Billy," he screams, "The fumes!"

The lighter clicks again and this time it lights.

CHAPTER FIFTY-TWO

BELLA

Dear God, dear God, this can't be happening. If I force myself, I'll wake up. If I concentrate, I'll wake up in my own bed in my own home and this nightmare will go away. This cannot be happening. I'm hanging in the air, hovering. There's a roaring sound like the sea in my ears and a pounding in my chest like waves crashing against rocks. Then there's the pain. It begins like pressure constricting my chest, then it grows to a crushing, gripping agony and I can't inhale. I'm falling, falling. Someone is holding my head, people are moving around me. I stare straight ahead unable to move. I stare straight ahead at the burning cross.

Is this the end, I wonder? I expected a cascade of flowers not a trial by fire. Is this how it ends?

CHAPTER FIFTY-THREE

MELANIE

I'm standing too close to the fire and I can't move. My face is sore from the heat and I can't move. My eyes are streaming from the smoke or maybe I'm crying. I don't want to burn. I want to run away but I'm paralyzed, I'm glued to the spot and the heat is burning me. I inhale a lungful of the searing heat and manage to exhale a scream. Every breath exhales a scream until Jez slaps my face and I'm released.

I back away unable to take in what's happening, is Billy under the flames? Is Billy still there or is the fire just burning itself? I can't see him. I can't see anything but fire. Jez is running, he is running hard away from the fire and I follow him. I manage to make myself move and I walk away, then I run. I run from the bus stop and the fire and my past. I run after Jez and into my future.

CHAPTER FIFTY-FOUR

JEZ

There's a whoosh then a roar and the heat is awful. Billy makes no sound. He doesn't move. He stands there for a moment or two with his arms outstretched like some grotesque fiery cross. The smell of burning petrol stings my eyes. I can't believe what I'm seeing. Nobody moves or makes a sound. It's as if time stands still. Suddenly there's screaming but it is not coming from Billy. He is silent. Melanie is screaming and screaming and I can't bear the sound. I slap her face to shut her up. An old biddy has collapsed and my teacher is fussing round her like a mother hen.

Billy keels forward and lies face down in the gutter. Now everybody seems to be staring at me, blaming me.

"It's not my fault," I keep repeating. "It's not my fault. It was the fumes that ignited. I didn't mean it to happen. He was annoying me. He was annoying everyone, but I didn't want him to be hurt, I didn't want him to die."

They say nothing they just stare.

I turn and run and run until I can't get a breath. I

stand, doubled-up, gasping on the pavement, then I see I'm outside a church and I stagger through the open door. I collapse into a pew and sit with my head in my hands. The church is cold and dark and smells of decades of despair. I don't know how long I sit here, but nobody disturbs me. Then, all of a sudden, I'm aware of sunlight flooding through the open door, it seems to run through the church like a line of fire. It illuminates the altar and the large cross facing me. A wave of despair washes over me and I stand to leave. That's when I see her. That's when I see my angel and it all makes perfect sense.

CHAPTER FIFTY-FIVE

DAVID

"Billy, the fumes," I yell "The fumes will ignite." But I'm too late to save him. It was always too late to save him. I stare in horror as he burns. He is burning and there is nothing anyone can do. He is burning and my sins are burning with him.

The woman beside me has collapsed and I'm cradling her head and trying to comfort her. By the time Billy keels forward into the gutter everyone has gone or is running away and I'm stuck here on my own. What the hell do I do? I'm stuck here on my own with two dying people. Is this what Hell is like? Is Hell being alone in a nightmare unable to leave and unable to summon for help? Is this the wrath of God? How do I atone for this?

Dear Lord surely this isn't the price of salvation.

EPILOGUE

For those who wish to know what happened next, allow me to enlighten you. Billy's Mum and his Aunty Mabel, after grieving for him for an appropriate time, spend their lives enjoying the money from his estate. This was no small sum. Mr. Henderson, believing Billy might be his son, set up an endowment policy in his name with a guaranteed life cover of £100,000. The last time I heard, Billy's Mum and his Aunty Mabel were holidaying in The Bahamas.

Witnessing Billy's awful death caused Bella Worthington to have a heart attack. The paramedics eventually arrived and put her in an ambulance where she complained all the way to the hospital about their incompetence. In this instance, she was right as she was dead on arrival at the casualty department.

David quit his boring job and much to the delight of his parents, moved to Israel. It's lucky they don't know the whole truth. It's lucky they don't know he re-invented himself as 'Tofu' the most sensational gay, porn star the country has ever known.

Jez and Melanie got religion in a manner of speaking. They disappeared for a few months, only to re-emerge in the United States as Jeremiah Church and his beautiful wife, Angel. They make millions of dollars out of a 'pay for view' evangelical show and are more famous than the president.

And what became of Billy? He dreamt of being a Superhero, of leaving his mark in the world, but like a candle in the wind, his life was snuffed out in a flash. Then Billy skipped happily towards the pearly gates to be welcomed with open arms, his minor misdemeanours all forgiven. He did, however, achieve his goal. Billy left his mark for all to see because burned into the road, in front of the bus stop, is an outline where his body lay. For a long time after the event, people came to look at it and gossip about his spectacular demise. Billy's 'X', for the immediate future at least, will mark his spot.

ABOUT THE AUTHORS

Elly Grant is an accomplished author who's won a string of awards and commendations for her writing. She specialises in crime, and her Death in the Pyrenees series, set in a small spa town in French Catalonia, gives a real flavour of the delights and quirkiness of the region.

Elly lives much of her life in a small French town in the Eastern Pyrenees where she's an active member of the community, participating in local events. She takes inspiration from the way of life and the colourful characters she comes across. She doesn't have to search very hard to find things to write about and living in the most prolific wine producing region in France makes the task so much more delightful.

* * *

To learn more about Elly Grant, Angi Fox and discover more Next Chapter authors, visit our website at www.nextchapter.pub.

But Billy Can't Fly
ISBN: 978-4-82412-664-1
Mass Market

Published by
Next Chapter
1-60-20 Minami-Otsuka
170-0005 Toshima-Ku, Tokyo
+818035793528

14th February 2022

www.ingramcontent.com/pod-product-compliance
Lightning Source LLC
LaVergne TN
LVHW032009070526
838202LV00059B/6364